Current Controversies

Reparations for Black Americans

Other Books in the Current Controversies Series

Attacks on Science
Big Tech and Democracy
The Capitol Riot: Fragile Democracy
Cyberterrorism
Domestic Extremism
Domestic vs. Offshore Manufacturing
Fossil Fuel Industries and the Green Economy
Hate Groups
The Internet of Things
Libertarians, Socialists, and Other Third Parties
The Politics and Science of COVID-19
Sustainable Consumption

Current Controversies

Reparations for Black Americans

Andrew Karpan, Book Editor

GREENHAVEN PUBLISHING

Published in 2022 by Greenhaven Publishing, LLC
353 3rd Avenue, Suite 255, New York, NY 10010

First Edition

Articles in Greenhaven Publishing anthologies are often edited for length to meet page requirements. In addition, original titles of these works are changed to clearly present the main thesis and to explicitly indicate the author's opinion. Every effort is made to ensure that Greenhaven Publishing accurately reflects the original intent of the authors. Every effort has been made to trace the owners of the copyrighted material.

Cover image: Boris Mayer/Shutterstock.com

Library of Congress Cataloging-in-Publication Data

Names: Karpan, Andrew, editor.
Title: Reparations for Black Americans / Andrew Karpan, book editor.
Description: First edition. | New York : Greenhaven Publishing, [2022] | Series: Current controversies | Includes bibliographical references and index. | Contents: Can reparations repair our collective injuries? — Would reparations have a positive economic impact? — Have reparations succeeded in the past? — Can reparations solve larger, systemic issues?| Audience: Ages 15+ | Audience: Grades 10–12 |Summary: "Anthology of diverse essays exploring the debate surrounding reparations for Black Americans as compensation for the horrors of slavery in the US as well as generations of damaging policies that have impeded the development of African American communities. Experts from the field debate whether reparations are necessary, if they could ever be sufficient, and how they could be implemented"— Provided by publisher.
Identifiers: LCCN 2021035633 | ISBN 9781534508538 (library binding) | ISBN 9781534508521 (paperback) | ISBN 9781534508545 (ebook)
Subjects: LCSH: African Americans—Reparations. | Reparations for historical injustices—Case studies.
Classification: LCC E185.89.R45 R474 2022 | DDC 305.896/073—dc23
LC record available at https://lccn.loc.gov/2021035633

Manufactured in the United States of America

Website: http://greenhavenpublishing.com

Contents

Foreword 12

Introduction 15

Chapter 1: Can Reparations Repair Our Collective Injuries?

Overview: A Brief History of Slavery Reparation Promises 19

John Torpey

The notion of compensating formerly enslaved people has existed since at least the time of the Civil War, but reparations for Black Americans has never really gained traction until recently. Americans are polarized on the issue, so an inquiry into the matter must be undertaken in order to gain bipartisan support.

Yes: Reparations Are a Legally Precedented Method of Redressing Historical Harm

Reparations Could Help an American Dream Deferred 24

Rashawn Ray and Andre M. Perry

Reparations are a solution aimed at a historic level of inequality: living side by side in the same country, the average white family still has roughly ten times the amount of wealth as the average Black family. Since the myth of "bootstrapping" isn't going to erase racial wealth divides, reparations should come in the form of wealth-building opportunities that directly address racial disparities in education, housing, and business ownership.

This Is an Opportunity to Lead by Example 34

Anne C. Bailey

Beginning a formal process of reparations would alter America's image of itself as well as provide a model for redressing historical injustices around the world. The United States is nowhere near the only country with a history of unaddressed human rights abuses, but it can be one of the few countries in the world that truly addresses these wrongs.

There Is a Moral Obligation to Reparations 38

Carissa Véliz

The reparations debate asks us to ask ourselves what we owe for the wrongs of history and how much our system has benefited from what is understood to have been as morally wrong as it was illegal, a form of theft carried out over generations and only compounded with time. Enslaved people worked and produced for others without getting anything in return: the fruits of their work were stolen by a system of forceful theft.

No: Reparations Will Never Succeed in Righting the Wrongs of Slavery

There Is No Legal Case for Reparations **42**

Luke Moffett

When reparations have been successful in the past, it was when survivors were still alive or there was sufficient evidence to find a responsible actor to make reparations. At this point, reparations cannot provide a complete solution. No amount of money, memorial, or apology can fully remedy the past.

Reparations Are Unaffordable and Ethically Disastrous **46**

Graham Hillard

In addition to doing little for the pain of its recipients, reparations would be ethically disastrous. They would invite endless litigation and subject Americans to the spectacle of government officials deciding who counts as Black or white.

Reparations May Be a Moral Imperative, but They Are Also a Political Disaster **49**

Francis Wilkinson

Exploring ways in which Black Americans were denied access to government programs that elevated whites into the middle class would be educational, but more people need to be educated. Historical knowledge has rarely been Americans' strong suit, and many schools do a poor job teaching about slavery and the struggle for civil rights.

Chapter 2: Would Reparations Have a Positive Economic Impact?

Overview: There Are Many Ways of Building Wealth **54**

Raina Zhao

The prospect of reparations takes many forms and need not be limited to lump sum payments. The idea of reparations, as it were, involves finding ways to create new sources of Black wealth and repair the human rights abuses that have deliberately prevented it from accumulating. These can include everything from public trust funds to baby bonds.

Yes: Reparations Would Redistribute Economic Resources to Groups That Have Been Historically Marginalized by the Current Distribution of Capital

Industrial Policy Will Truly Address the Legacy of Slavery **59**

Samuel Hammond

Reparations in the form of a direct payment risks trivializing slavery as merely an issue of stolen labor. To address the lack of development that occurred for generations as a result of this colonization, African American communities need investments in infrastructure and a strategy for developing a high-wage workforce.

Black-Led Resistance Movements Are Paving the Way for Reparations **64**

Sarah Freeman-Woolpert

Activists in the United States and around the world are using 2020's social justice movements as a way to move the reparations debate forward. In this interview, Truth Telling Project codirector David Ragland discusses the four Rs of reparations: resistance, repentance, restitution, and reconciliation.

Voluntary Reparations Should Be Supported by Everyone **69**

Theodore Kalambokidis

While reparations remains a contentious issue in the United States, voluntary reparations would be an effective first step. Under a system of voluntary reparations, anybody could choose whether or not to fund the reparations payments, much like a charitable donation. The author presents a case for how this might be achieved.

No: Reparations Aren't Economically Feasible

Cash Reparations Won't Work **73**

Corey Walker

Reparations in the form of cash payouts—very often the form in which they're immediately discussed—are politically unpopular and would likely not have lasting success. In fact, history has shown that when wealth is given out randomly, descendants often have no better outcomes in wealth or education than the descendants of others.

Reparations Won't Solve America's Race Problem 77

Stefan Spath

Acknowledging the injustice of slavery, the author argues that it would be nearly impossible to determine who should be compensated and how. Paying money to Black Americans won't stimulate the economy, and legislation already has righted past wrongs. A better solution to racial inequality is a commitment to individualism.

Cash Payments Hurt Those Who Receive Them 85

Robert Rector and Mimi Teixeira

The history of solving larger economic problems by using cash payments generally hurt the people who are given them. Instead, it makes people dependent on those payments but does little to change their larger economic situation.

Chapter 3: Have Reparations Succeeded in the Past?

Overview: Reparations Worked Before—Just the Other Way Around 91

Thomas Craemer

When a slave revolt led to the end of French rule over Haiti, France demanded the new country compensate former slave owners for the loss of what was deemed their property, a program that continued until 1947, with the money going to more than 7,900 former slave owners and their descendants in France. It's not the only instance of how the logic of reparations worked in the past and suggests a different way of looking at the present debate.

Yes: Reparations Have Been Successful in the Past

How Reparations Worked Between Germany and Israel 95

Lily Gardner Feldman

In 1952, only a few years after both the end of World War II and the Holocaust and the creation of the State of Israel, Germany and Israel came to an agreement that involved a payment of the equivalent of $7 billion today. A look at how that deal came to be sheds light on how reparations can work. Since that payment, the two countries have enjoyed a close diplomatic relationship, something that could not have been envisioned sixty years ago.

The US Has Issued Reparations Before 101

Rhoda E. Howard-Hassmann

One of the major instances in American history when the federal government distributed reparations was to the 120,000 Japanese Americans who were imprisoned without cause during World War II. This occurred in 1988, and the amount paid was relatively low, $20,000 for each of 80,000 living survivors, for a total of about $1.6 billion.

No: When Tried, Reparations Have Largely Failed

Reparations After World War I Failed to a Disastrous Degree 105

The Historian of the US Department of State

After the end of World War I, countries in Europe saddled Germany with immense payments they demanded to be paid in reparations, a situation that led to the country's economy collapsing numerous times in the decade ahead. The United States tried twice to intervene, but both efforts eventually failed in the wake of the global economic crisis that it had its own hand in helping to start.

South Africa's Reparations Program Has Been a Disappointment 109

Ashley Ridge

Another reparations project was the Truth and Reconciliation Commission, which was started by the South African government in 1995, following the end of apartheid rule over that country. In the time since, the reparations that the group have meted out have been met with scrutiny: Why do some people receive compensation, but not others? Why are some events of human suffering more worthy of aid than others?

Chapter 4: Can Reparations Solve Larger, Systemic Issues?

Overview: Reparations Could Narrow the Racial Wealth Gap 122

Terry Gross

Reparations are part of the larger story of finding a way of ending racism in America, and the debate around them often serves as a proxy for how people feel racism has impacted their lives.

The distribution of wealth is just one facet of it. Passed through, generation by generation, it reflects the economic impacts of injustice and suggests ways that can be discussed.

Yes: Reparations Are a Vital and Moral Part of Responding to Systemic Inequalities

Reparations Are Necessary, but So Is Even More **128**

Bhaskar Sunkara

In debating reparations, we are really debating how to economically transform sectors of American life that have been denied the same opportunities as its millions of fellow Americans. This is why supporters need to look beyond the idea of sorting out how reparations will work and turn, instead, to how society can be better organized in a more fair and just way.

How Reparations Can Make Us Whole **133**

Shmuly Yanklowitz

What reparations are ultimately about are our debts: the debts that slavery has forced on the enslaved and the slaveholders alike. Policies framed in that light are about finding a larger way that our society's ills can be confronted and repaired. Only in this way can we ever live in a society that is just.

Reparations Are an Idea Whose Time Has Come **136**

Joyce Hope Scott

This moment, in particular, has attracted the larger debate about reparations, as the lens of iPhones, nightly reports by the media, the Black Lives Matter movement, protests against extrajudicial powers of the police, and the murder of Black people with impunity has exposed the fragile underbelly of our society. What's been revealed is structural racism and visceral inequality.

No: Reparations Will Do Little to Change the Lives of Those They Are Directed At

Reparations Are Too Messy to Work **141**

Stuart E. Eizenstat

Reparations generally work when the crime was recent and the direct victims are still alive. Without those factors, it's hard to convince either side that they will be satisfied by the arrangement. Restitution has come from the direct perpetrators of the crimes and has to go largely to those who directly suffered and survived, and, in some cases, their heirs.

Can Reparations Correct Something Like the Tulsa Massacre? **149**

Mihir Desai and Brian Kenny

This excerpted interview unpacks the totality of loss that occurs as a result of a violent act like the Tulsa Massacre. Such loss is ultimately incalculable and, as time passes, the validity of those claims feels less like financial losses and more like a matter of history.

As a Legal Process, Reparations Will Never Happen **157**

Darren Zook

This excerpted viewpoint argues that it's difficult to see how reparations would fit in under the current organization of common law. This is because the law cannot be applied retroactively, as in, the act in question had to be illegal by the laws in place at the time it was committed to be considered a crime.

Organizations to Contact **162**

Bibliography **167**

Index **171**

Foreword

"Controversy" is a word that has an undeniably unpleasant connotation. It carries a definite negative charge. Controversy can spoil family gatherings, spread a chill around classroom and campus discussion, inflame public discourse, open raw civic wounds, and lead to the ouster of public officials. We often feel that controversy is almost akin to bad manners, a rude and shocking eruption of that which must not be spoken or thought of in polite, tightly guarded society. To avoid controversy, to quell controversy, is often seen as a public good, a victory for etiquette, perhaps even a moral or ethical imperative.

Yet the studious, deliberate avoidance of controversy is also a whitewashing, a denial, a death threat to democracy. It is a false sterilizing and sanitizing and superficial ordering of the messy, ragged, chaotic, at times ugly processes by which a healthy democracy identifies and confronts challenges, engages in passionate debate about appropriate approaches and solutions, and arrives at something like a consensus and a broadly accepted and supported way forward. Controversy is the megaphone, the speaker's corner, the public square through which the citizenry finds and uses its voice. Controversy is the life's blood of our democracy and absolutely essential to the vibrant health of our society.

Our present age is certainly no stranger to controversy. We are consumed by fierce debates about technology, privacy, political correctness, poverty, violence, crime and policing, guns, immigration, civil and human rights, terrorism, militarism, environmental protection, and gender and racial equality. Loudly competing voices are raised every day, shouting opposing opinions, putting forth competing agendas, and summoning starkly different visions of a utopian or dystopian future. Often these voices attempt to shout the others down; there is precious little listening and considering among the cacophonous din.

Yet listening and considering, too, are essential to the health of a democracy. If controversy is democracy's lusty lifeblood, respectful listening and careful thought are its higher faculties, its brain, its conscience.

Current Controversies does not shy away from or attempt to hush the loudly competing voices. It seeks to provide readers with as wide and representative as possible a range of articulate voices on any given controversy of the day, separates each one out to allow it to be heard clearly and fairly, and encourages careful listening to each of these well-crafted, thoughtfully expressed opinions, supplied by some of today's leading academics, thinkers, analysts, politicians, policy makers, economists, activists, change agents, and advocates. Only after listening to a wide range of opinions on an issue, evaluating the strengths and weaknesses of each argument, assessing how well the facts and available evidence mesh with the stated opinions and conclusions, and thoughtfully and critically examining one's own beliefs and conscience can the reader begin to arrive at his or her own conclusions and articulate his or her own stance on the spotlighted controversy.

This process is facilitated and supported in each Current Controversies volume by an introduction and chapter overviews that provide readers with the essential context they need to begin engaging with the spotlighted controversies, with the debates surrounding them, and with their own perhaps shifting or nascent opinions on them. Chapters are organized around several key questions that are answered with diverse opinions representing all points on the political spectrum. In its content, organization, and methodology, readers are encouraged to determine the authors' point of view and purpose, interrogate and analyze the various arguments and their rhetoric and structure, evaluate the arguments' strengths and weaknesses, test their claims against available facts and evidence, judge the validity of the reasoning, and bring into clearer, sharper focus the reader's own beliefs and conclusions and how they may differ from or align with those in the collection or those of classmates.

Research has shown that reading comprehension skills improve dramatically when students are provided with compelling, intriguing, and relevant "discussable" texts. The subject matter of these collections could not be more compelling, intriguing, or urgently relevant to today's students and the world they are poised to inherit. The anthologized articles also provide the basis for stimulating, lively, and passionate classroom debates. Students who are compelled to anticipate objections to their own argument and identify the flaws in those of an opponent read more carefully, think more critically, and steep themselves in relevant context, facts, and information more thoroughly. In short, using discussable text of the kind provided by every single volume in the Current Controversies series encourages close reading, facilitates reading comprehension, fosters research, strengthens critical thinking, and greatly enlivens and energizes classroom discussion and participation. The entire learning process is deepened, extended, and strengthened.

If we are to foster a knowledgeable, responsible, active, and engaged citizenry, we must provide readers with the intellectual, interpretive, and critical-thinking tools and experience necessary to make sense of the world around them and of the all-important debates and arguments that inform it. We must encourage them not to run away from or attempt to quell controversy but to embrace it in a responsible, conscientious, and thoughtful way, to sharpen and strengthen their own informed opinions by listening to and critically analyzing those of others. This series encourages respectful engagement with and analysis of current controversies and competing opinions and fosters a resulting increase in the strength and rigor of one's own opinions and stances. As such, it helps readers assume their rightful place in the public square and provides them with the skills necessary to uphold their awesome responsibility—guaranteeing the continued and future health of a vital, vibrant, and free democracy.

Introduction

> *"One cannot escape the question by hand-waving at the past, disavowing the acts of one's ancestors, nor by citing a recent date of ancestral immigration. The last slaveholder has been dead for a very long time. The last soldier to endure Valley Forge has been dead much longer. To proudly claim the veteran and disown the slaveholder is patriotism à la carte."*
>
> *—Ta-Nehisi Coates*[1]

The debate over what, if anything, America owes the millions of people held hostage here for most of its history dates to the very end of slavery. In early 1865, General William Tecumseh Sherman signed Field Order 15, a document approved by President Abraham Lincoln that formally confiscated about 400,000 acres of land in the rebel states of South Carolina, Georgia, and Florida and distributed it among approximately 18,000 people who had been enslaved.

This was not an uncommon way to deal with land in that era: the Homestead Act, passed by Congress three years earlier, had allowed 1.6 million people who had not taken up arms against the country in the ongoing Civil War to split more than 160 million acres of land in the American West among themselves, an act of large-scale wealth redistribution that's largely responsible for the phenomenon of the small and well-to-do American town. "The islands from Charleston south, the abandoned rice-fields along the rivers for thirty miles back from the sea, and the country bordering the Saint Johns River, Florida, are reserved and set apart for the settlement of the Blacks now made free by the acts of war and the proclamation of the President of the United States," the first line of the order read.

But the Field Order was not to be. A few months later, Lincoln was assassinated and his replacement, Andrew Johnson, issued his own proclamation returning the land to its former owners, in exchange for signing a loyalty oath. The formerly enslaved were given nothing, and the shadow of debt hung instead over the political landscape.

The notion of direct reparations was never lost in the century and a half that followed. Activists such as Audley Moore and James Forman made it central to their platforms, and in 1993, the NAACP formally endorsed the program. In every session of Congress for more than twenty-five years, the late congressman John Conyers Jr. endorsed a bill calling for the subject to be studied.

The latest incarnation of this debate was sparked by the writer Ta-Nehisi Coates, whose essay "The Case for Reparations," published in *The Atlantic* magazine in 2014, created a new language to articulate that debt, one that became a ubiquitous subtext in the conversations surrounding the Black Lives Matter movement, which itself dates to 2013:

> Our concerns are rooted not in the impracticality of reparations but in something more existential. If we conclude that the conditions in […] black America are not inexplicable but are instead precisely what you'd expect of a community that for centuries has lived in America's crosshairs, then what are we to make of the world's oldest democracy?"[2]

Coates's essay laid out the case that the issue had come down to the fundamental promise of American democracy and the sense of opportunity that animated it. It was the same debate that animated the country's primary political movement during its first century, the abolitionist fight to end slavery in the country.

Coming toward the end of the second term of the country's first Black president, the new movement suggested that there were inequalities in modern life that could not be answered by the symbolic language of modern politics and that have done little to blunt the impact of centuries of inequality. Reparations became a new way to think about how wealth in American society was distributed and to contemplate how different the country would look if it were organized another way.

As an idea, reparations presented a mechanism to imagine the future differently, too, and its language spread far outside the discourse of Black lives in America. At the turn of the most recent decade, a climate reporter at the *New Republic* would ask if carbon removal could be purposed as a direct form of "climate reparations."[3]

Despite Coates's urging, the response to calls for reparations has been one of impracticality. It is, namely, too expensive. Efforts to estimate the price tag of such an effort easily go to the trillions, a number its supporters largely do not focus on disputing. To do so would have the effect of dismissing the urgency of the very cause. The impact of slavery on the enslaved feels, largely and reasonable so, beyond accounting.

But to account for history is in the very nature of debating about it, and the viewpoints in *Current Controversies: Reparations for Black Americans* do just that. In diverging perspectives, viewpoint authors examine the turns that the current debate over reparations have taken and look to history to take account of when reparations have been tried in the past. Some have failed; others have succeeded. Ultimately, like the arguments that follow, they make an effort to plot a path forward, through a future that never forgets its past.

Endnotes

1. Ta-Nehisi Coates, "The Case for Reparations," *The Atlantic*, June 15, 2014.
2. Coates, "The Case for Reparations."
3. Kate Aronoff, "Carbon Capture Is Not a Climate Savior," *The New Republic*, December 24, 2020.

Current Controversies

Chapter 1

Can Reparations Repair Our Collective Injuries?

Overview: A Brief History of Slavery Reparation Promises

John Torpey

John Torpey is professor of sociology and history and director of the Ralph Bunche Institute for International Studies at the Graduate Center, CUNY. He is the author or editor of a number of books, including Making Whole What Has Been Smashed: On Reparations Politics *(2006).*

Does the United States owe descendants of slaves reparations? It's a question being asked more frequently of Democrats running for the 2020 presidential nomination. Many have expressed varying degrees of support for reparations, giving the idea the greatest prominence it's ever had among leading politicians.

Although the notion of compensating freed slaves has been around since at least the Civil War, providing reparations for their descendants has never really gained much traction in the United States, as I learned while researching my book *Making Whole What Has Been Smashed.*

Is anything different now?

Reparations Are Rare

Historically, the term "reparations" dealt primarily with the indemnification of states ravaged by war, such as those required of the Germans by the Versailles Treaty after World War I.

In the aftermath of World War II, however, the term began to acquire a broader meaning, extending to compensation for those injured by the actions of a state.

Still, such compensation has happened only rarely.

Germany paid Holocaust survivors US$927 million—or $8.84 billion today—in compensation as part of the 1952 Luxembourg Agreement, most of it going to the newly created state of Israel to defray the costs of resettlement.

Later, the US offered "redress" to some 82,000 Japanese Americans who were incarcerated as "enemy aliens" during World War II. The 1988 Civil Liberties Act granted a presidential apology and $20,000 to each living person who had been detained based on the recommendations of a commission created by Congress in 1980 to examine the causes of the "internment."

But this payback was intended to be very limited. During the debate, then-Sen. Ernest Hollings worried, "Where do we draw the line against reparations to the countless other groups of Americans who have suffered because of actions of the US government?"

And the law explicitly says compensation would only be provided to victims still alive in order to preclude reparations claims by the descendants of black slaves and others.

"40 Acres and a Mule"

Efforts to avoid establishing a precedent for reparations arose in part because former slaves and their descendants have long sought some sort of compensation for their suffering under slavery and segregation. These efforts have achieved little.

Perhaps the best-known measure intended to get blacks on their feet after the Civil War was General William Sherman's promise of land and loaned mules to work it.

Yet after taking office in 1865, President Andrew Johnson rescinded efforts to distribute land to those who were freed. Scholar-activist W. E. B. Du Bois thus observed that "the vision of 'forty acres and a mule' … was destined in most cases to bitter disappointment."

"Freedom Is Not Enough"

A century after the Civil War, however, President Lyndon Johnson hinted at the need for reparations when he pushed through civil rights legislation intended to make blacks full citizens.

During a speech at Howard University in 1965, he declared: "Freedom is not enough. … It is not enough just to open the gates of opportunity."

Although Johnson didn't call explicitly for reparations, he urged something more than just equal rights for blacks—something that would rectify the economic disadvantage blacks faced. The speech has often been seen as a harbinger of affirmative action.

Two years later, in the aftermath of urban riots in Newark, Detroit and elsewhere, Johnson created the Kerner Commission to investigate the causes and recommend remedies. The commission found that "white racism" was the basic cause of the racial unrest and proposed massive investment in black communities.

Although the report was a best-seller, Johnson found the conclusions politically distasteful and distanced himself from the commission.

Martin Luther King Jr. agreed with these critical assessments of black deprivation, but generally couched his appeals for addressing poverty in interracial terms. King did once indicate that he was coming to Washington "for a check," but this was a rare aside.

The heart of King's "Poor People's Campaign," his main focus toward the end of his life, was a universal basic income, not reparations.

But others would pick up the reparations baton. Black radical James Forman, for example, stormed Manhattan's famously progressive Riverside Church in May 1969 to demand $500 million from "the white Christian churches and Jewish synagogues that are part and parcel of the capitalist system." This and other demands formed the basis of the Black National Economic Conference's "Black Manifesto."

Calls for a Commission

Little came of these efforts until decades later when then-Congressman John Conyers introduced the first bill on the issue in 1989.

It proposed a commission to "study and consider a national apology and proposal for reparations for the institution of slavery, its subsequent de jure and de facto racial and economic discrimination against African Americans, and the impact of these forces on living African Americans, [and] to make recommendations to the Congress on appropriate remedies."

The Commission to Study Reparation Proposals for African Americans Act has been proposed in every legislature since and never garnered much support. Even during President Barack Obama's tenure in the Oval Office, little changed, despite the appearance of author Ta-Nehisi Coates' much-discussed 2014 plea for reparations.

Indeed, shortly before he left office, Obama told Coates that, as a political matter, reparations for black people was far less likely than a "progressive program for lifting up all people."

Different This Time?

Heading into 2020, some believe that the time for reparations may have come.

A driving force behind the persistence of reparations is just how stark the racial differences remain. Relative to whites, blacks tend to have lower educational attainment, rates of home ownership and life expectancy but higher rates of poverty, incarceration, unemployment and life-threatening diseases. The wealth gap between whites and blacks is very large, and wage inequality is likely making it worse.

But are all these disparities rooted in slavery and segregation? This is where a congressional inquiry, which may finally be politically palatable thanks to the growing embrace of the idea among prominent Democrats, would come in.

Success, which will require legislation, will depend on building bipartisan support for the inquiry. Accordingly, I believe it's best to avoid talk of "reparations." After all, most Americans oppose them and always have.

First, get the commission and let it determine the causes of racial inequalities and the form that remedies should take. As poverty is not an affliction of blacks alone, the US must also address the poverty that affects many others as well.

If the commission is given the opportunity to explore the causes of and remedies for racial inequality, however, perhaps Americans can finally move toward rectifying the inequities that beset blacks as a result of their country's history of slavery, segregation and discrimination.

Reparations Could Help an American Dream Deferred

Rashawn Ray and Andre M. Perry

Rashawn Ray is a professor of sociology at the University of Maryland and is the author of a 2010 book titled Race and Ethnic Relations in the 21st Century: History, Theory, Institutions, and Policy. *Andre M. Perry is the author of a book called* Know Your Price: Valuing Black Lives and Property in America's Black Cities *and runs a consulting company.*

Central to the idea of the American Dream lies an assumption that we all have an equal opportunity to generate the kind of wealth that brings meaning to the words "life, liberty and the pursuit of happiness," boldly penned in the Declaration of Independence. The American Dream portends that with hard work, a person can own a home, start a business, and grow a nest egg for generations to draw upon. This belief, however, has been defied repeatedly by the United States government's own decrees that denied wealth-building opportunities to Black Americans.

Today, the average white family has roughly 10 times the amount of wealth as the average Black family. White college graduates have over seven times more wealth than Black college graduates. Making the American Dream an equitable reality demands the same US government that denied wealth to Blacks restore that deferred wealth through reparations to their descendants in the form of individual cash payments in the amount that will close the Black-white racial wealth divide. Additionally, reparations should come in the form of wealth-building opportunities that address racial disparities in education, housing, and business ownership.

In 1860, over $3 billion was the value assigned to the physical bodies of enslaved Black Americans to be used as free labor and

"Why We Need Reparations for Black Americans," by Rashawn Ray and Andre M. Perry, brookings.edu, April 15, 2020. Reprinted by permission.

production. This was more money than was invested in factories and railroads combined. In 1861, the value placed on cotton produced by enslaved Blacks was $250 million. Slavery enriched white slave owners and their descendants, and it fueled the country's economy while suppressing wealth building for the enslaved. The United States has yet to compensate descendants of enslaved Black Americans for their labor. Nor has the federal government atoned for the lost equity from anti-Black housing, transportation, and business policy. Slavery, Jim Crow segregation, anti-Black practices like redlining, and other discriminatory public policies in criminal justice and education have robbed Black Americans of the opportunities to build wealth (defined as assets minus debt) afforded to their white peers.

Bootstrapping isn't going to erase racial wealth divides. As economists William "Sandy" Darity and Darrick Hamilton point out in their 2018 report, *What We Get Wrong About Closing the Wealth Gap*, "Blacks cannot close the racial wealth gap by changing their individual behavior—i.e. by assuming more 'personal responsibility' or acquiring the portfolio management insights associated with '[financial] literacy.'" In fact, white high school dropouts have more wealth than Black college graduates. Moreover, the racial wealth gap did not result from a lack of labor. Rather, it came from a lack of financial capital.

Not only do racial wealth disparities reveal fallacies in the American Dream, the financial and social consequences are significant and wide-ranging. Wealth is positively correlated with better health, educational, and economic outcomes. Furthermore, assets from homes, stocks, bonds, and retirement savings provide a financial safety net for the inevitable shocks to the economy and personal finances that happen throughout a person's lifespan.

Recessions impact everyone, but wealth is distributed quite unevenly in the US. The woeful inadequacy of a government-sponsored safety net was made apparent in the wake of economic disasters like the 2008 housing crisis and natural ones like Hurricane Katrina in 2005. Those who can draw upon the equity in a home, savings, and securities are able to recover faster after economic downturns than those without wealth. The lack of a social safety net and the racial wealth divide are currently on display amid the COVID-19 crisis. Disparities in access to health care along with inequities in economic policies combine to make Black people more vulnerable to negative consequences than white individuals.

Below, we provide a history of reparations in the United States, missed opportunities to redress the racial wealth gap, and specific details of a viable reparations package for Black Americans.

History of Reparations in the United States

Reparations—a system of redress for egregious injustices—are not foreign to the United States. Native Americans have received land and billions of dollars for various benefits and programs for being forcibly exiled from their native lands. For Japanese Americans, $1.5 billion was paid to those who were interned during World War II. Additionally, the United States, via the Marshall Plan, helped to ensure that Jews received reparations for the Holocaust, including making various investments over time. In 1952, West Germany agreed to pay 3.45 billion Deutsche Marks to Holocaust survivors.

Black Americans are the only group that has not received reparations for state-sanctioned racial discrimination, while slavery afforded some white families the ability to accrue tremendous wealth. And, we must note that American slavery was particularly brutal. About 15 percent of the enslaved shipped from Western Africa died during transport. The enslaved were regularly beaten and lynched for frivolous infractions. Slavery also disrupted families as one in three marriages were split up and one in five children were separated from their parents. The case for reparations can be made on economic, social, and moral grounds. The United States had multiple opportunities to atone for slavery—each a missed chance to make the American Dream a reality—but has yet to undertake significant action.

Missed Policy Opportunities to Atone for Slavery with Reparations

40 Acres and a Mule

The first major opportunity that the United States had and where it should have atoned for slavery was right after the Civil War. Union leaders including General William Sherman concluded that each Black family should receive 40 acres. Sherman signed Field Order 15 and allocated 400,000 acres of confiscated Confederate land to Black families. Additionally, some families were to receive mules left over from the war, hence 40 acres and a mule.

Yet, after President Abraham Lincoln's assassination, President Andrew Johnson reversed Field Order 15 and returned land back to former slave owners. Instead of giving Blacks the means to support themselves, the federal government empowered former enslavers. For example, in Washington D.C., slave owners were actually paid reparations for lost property—the formally enslaved. This practice was also common in nearby states. Many Black Americans with limited work options returned as sharecroppers to till the same land for the very slave owners to whom they were once enslaved. Slave owners not only made money off the chattel enslavement of Black Americans, but they then made money multiple times over off the land that the formerly enslaved had no choice but to work.

The New Deal

There's never a bad time to do what's morally right, but the United States has had prime opportunities to atone for slavery. In the 1930s, the United States was reeling from the 1929 stock market crash and was firmly engulfed in the Great Depression. The Franklin Roosevelt administration implemented a series of policies as part of his New Deal legislation, estimated to cost roughly $50 billion then, to catapult the country out of depression. Current estimates price the New Deal at about $50 trillion.

Two particular policies of the New Deal fell short in redressing American's racial wrongs—the G.I. Bill and Social Security. Though white and Black Americans fought in WWII, Black veterans could not redeem their post-war benefits like their white peers. While the G.I. Bill was mandated federally, it was implemented locally. The presence of racial housing covenants and redlining among local municipalities prohibited Blacks from utilizing federal benefits. White soldiers were afforded the opportunity to build wealth by sending themselves and their children to college and by obtaining housing and small business grants.

Regarding Social Security, two key professions that would have improved equity in America were excluded from the legislation—domestic and farm workers. These omissions effectively excluded 60 percent of Blacks across the US and 75 percent in southern states who worked in these occupations. Roosevelt bargained these exclusionary provisions in the legislation on the backs of Black veterans and workers in order to propel mostly white America out of the Great Depression.

There are other policies and practices that contributed to racial wealth gap. Government-sanctioned discrimination related to the 1862 Homestead Act, redlining, restrictive covenants, and convict leasing blocked Blacks from the ability to gain wealth at similar rates as whites. Separate from slavery, damages should be awarded to Black people who were harmed by these policies and practices.

Reparations for Slavery and Anti-Black Policies

We know the monetary value that was placed on enslaved Blacks and the productivity of their labor, as well as the amount of the racial wealth gap. We've seen other groups receive restitutions while the federal government pulled back reparations for Black Americans. Accordingly, if we want to close the racial wealth gap and live up to our moral creed to protect "life, liberty and the pursuit of happiness," a federal reparations package for Black Americans is in order. This package should include individual and collective public benefits that simultaneously builds wealth and eliminates debt among Black citizens. We assert that it should be similar to the Harriet Tubman Community Investment

Act, which was recently heard before the Maryland General Assembly where Ray testified on its behalf. The Harriet Tubman Community Investment Act aims to atone for slavery and its legacy by addressing education, homeownership, and business ownership barriers.

Individual Payments for Descendants of Enslaved Black Americans

The US government owes lost wages as well as damages to the people it helped enslave. In addition to the lost wages, the accumulative amount of restitution for individuals should eliminate the racial wealth gap that currently exists. According to the Federal Reserve's most recent numbers in 2016, based on the Survey of Consumer Finances, white families had the highest median family wealth at $171,000, compared to Black and Hispanic families, which had $17,600 and $20,700, respectively.

College Tuition to 4-Year or 2-Year Colleges and Universities for Descendants of Enslaved Black Americans

People should be able to use the tuition remission to obtain a bachelor's degree or an associate's/vocational or technical degree. Tuition should be available for public or private universities. Considering the racial gap in the ability to obtain degrees at private schools, this part of the package will further help to reduce racial disparities by affording more social network access and opportunity structures.

Student Loan Forgiveness for Descendants of Enslaved Black Americans

Student loan debt continues to be a significant barrier to wealth creation for Black college graduates. Among 25-55 year olds, about 40 percent of Blacks compared to 30 percent of whites have student loan debt. Blacks also have nearly $45,000 of student loan debt compared to about $30,000 for whites. Recent research finds that Blacks are more likely to be allocated unsubsidized loans. Furthermore, graduates of Historically Black Colleges and

Universities, compared to Predominately White Institutions, are more likely to receive subprime loans with higher interest rates.

Universities including Georgetown and Princeton Theological Seminary, which is the second-oldest seminary in the country, are aiming to atone for the fact that the sale of slaves helped to fortify their university endowments and establish them as elite institutions of higher education on a global scale. Descendants of the slaves sold by Georgetown and Princeton Theological Seminary are now entitled to full rights and benefits bestowed by those universities to obtain degrees across the higher education pipeline. The Virginia state legislature voted for some of its state universities to atone for slavery with reparations. Other universities, along with state legislatures and the federal government, should follow suit.

Down Payment Grants and Housing Revitalization Grants for Descendants of Enslaved Black Americans

Down payment grants will provide Black Americans with some initial equity in their homes relative to mortgage insurance loans. Housing revitalization grants will help Black Americans to refurbish existing homes in neighborhoods that have been neglected due to a lack of government and corporate investments in predominately Black communities. Given recent settlements for predatory lending, low and fixed interest rates as well as property tax caps in areas in which housing prices are significantly devalued should be part of the package. After accounting for factors such as housing quality, neighborhood quality, education, and crime, owner-occupied homes in Black neighborhoods are undervalued by $48,000 per home on average, amounting to a whopping $156 billion that homeowners would have received if their homes were priced at market rates, according to Brookings research.

As gentrification occurs, Blacks are typically priced out of neighborhoods they helped to maintain, while the historical and current remnants of redlining and restrictive covenants inhibited investments. Some Black Americans are being forced from their family home of decades because of tax increases as neighborhoods are gentrified. This is an important point because some 2020 Democratic presidential candidates aimed to redress the racial wealth gap by focusing on historically redlined districts. Perry's research shows that these policies fall short of capturing a large segment of Black Americans.

Business Grants for Business Starting Up, Business Expansion to Hire More Employees, or Purchasing Property for Descendants of Enslaved Black Americans

Black-owned businesses are more likely to be located in predominately Black neighborhoods that need the infrastructure and businesses. However, Black business owners are still less likely to obtain capital from banks to make their businesses successful.

This reparations package for Black Americans is about restoring the wealth that has been extracted from Black people and communities. Still, reparations are all for naught without enforcement of anti-discrimination policies that remove barriers to economic mobility and wealth building. The architecture of the economy must change in order to create an equitable society. The racial wealth gap was created by racist policies. Federal intervention is needed to remove the racism that undergirds those polices. In some respects, the question of who should receive reparations is more controversial than what or how much people should be awarded.

Who Should Receive Reparations?

One key question after deciding what a reparations package should include is who should qualify. In short, a Black person who can trace their heritage to people enslaved in US states and territories should be eligible for financial compensation for slavery. Meanwhile, Black people who can show how they were excluded from various policies after emancipation should seek separate damages. For instance, a person like Senator Cory Booker whose parents are descendants of slaves would qualify for slavery reparations whereas Senator Kamala Harris (Jamaican immigrant father and Indian immigrant mother) and President Barack Obama (Kenyan immigrant father and white mother) may seek redress for housing and/or education segregation. Sasha and Malia Obama (whose mother is Michelle Robinson Obama, a descendant of enslaved Africans) would qualify.

To determine qualification, birth records can initially be used to determine if a person was classified as Black American. Economist Sandy Darity asserts that people should show a consistent pattern of identification. Census records can then be used to determine if a person has consistently identified as Black American. Finally, DNA testing can be used as a supplement to determine lineage. This is how Senator Booker, who first introduced a reparations bill in the Senate, learned that his lineage stemmed from Sierra Leone.

Conclusion

For the descendants of the 12.5 million Blacks who were shipped in chains from Western Africa, "America has a genetic birth defect when it comes to the question of race," as stated recently by US Representative Hakeem Jeffries. If America is to atone for this defect, reparations for Black Americans is part of the healing and reconciliation process.

With April 4 marking the fifty-second year since Dr. Martin Luther King Jr. was assassinated in Memphis, we think it is appropriate to end with an oft-forgotten quote from Dr. King's "I Have a Dream Speech" that he gave in 1963 in Washington, D.C. This statement is still one of the unfulfilled aspects of this policy-related speech:

> We have come to our nation's capital to cash a check. When the architects of our republic wrote the magnificent words of the Constitution and the Declaration of Independence, they were signing a promissory note to which every American was to fall heir. … It is obvious today that America has defaulted on this promissory note insofar as her citizens of color are concerned. Instead of honoring this sacred obligation, America has given the Negro people a bad check, a check which has come back

> marked "insufficient funds." But we refuse to believe that the bank of justice is bankrupt.

Given the lingering legacy of slavery on the racial wealth gap, the monetary value we know that was placed on enslaved Blacks, the fact that other groups have received reparations, and the fact that Blacks were originally awarded reparations only to have them rescinded provide overwhelming evidence that it is time to pay reparations to the descendants of enslaved Blacks.

This Is an Opportunity to Lead by Example

Anne C. Bailey

Anne C. Bailey is a professor of history at the State University of New York's Binghamton University and is the author of The Weeping Time: Memory and the Largest Slave Auction in American History.

Some 156 years after the end of the Civil War and the official abolition of slavery through the 13th Amendment, the idea of reparations is gaining currency in Washington.

On March 1, Cedric Richmond, a senior adviser to President Joe Biden, suggested the White House could "start acting now" on the issue. The comment comes just weeks after a House committee chaired by Rep. Sheila Jackson Lee, Democrat of Texas, heard testimony on H.R. 40, a bill that would establish a commission on the legacy of slavery that would look at possible payments for descendants of enslaved people of African descent.

Having researched slavery for the past three decades, I have concluded that there are many rationales for reparations. There has never been a leveling of the playing field, or payments for the debt of unpaid labor over 250 years of slavery. Furthermore, Black contribution to the wealth of America has not been acknowledged or given its due, in spite of the fact that the Southern planters and Northern manufacturers who helped shape the nation were made rich by turning raw commodities harvested by enslaved people into commercial empires.

But there is an additional reason that looking at reparations now makes sense. At a time when Biden is trying to rebuild America's image overseas, reparations for this unpaid debt could, I believe, drastically improve the United States' international standing and serve as an example to other nations on how to deal with past inequities.

A Promise Never Delivered

Campaigns for reparations have a long history. President Abraham Lincoln, who was known as "The Great Emancipator" in large part because he heeded the calls of Black abolitionists like ex-slave Frederick Douglass and signed the Emancipation Proclamation in 1863, was also a key advocate for a form of reparations.

Under Special Field Order No. 15, issued with Lincoln's blessing in 1865, newly emancipated slaves were to receive "forty acres and a mule."

Some freed slaves had already received their 40 acres at the time Congress passed the bill.

But this promise was not kept. After Lincoln was assassinated, President Andrew Johnson promptly vetoed the bill. According to noted economist William Darity, the cost of reneging on the promise to Black Americans was land worth more than US$1.3 trillion in today's dollars.

While efforts to compensate Black former slaves were thwarted, remarkably, some white slave owners seeking compensation for the end of slavery were more successful. Through 1862's District of Columbia Compensated Emancipation Act, slave owners were paid for their lost "property."

Debt Compounded

After the reversal of early efforts to compensate people of African descent, Southern states continued to put in place policies to maintain white supremacy.

What followed were decades of institutional marginalization under Jim Crow segregation that further impeded Black progress. Racist housing policies, employment practices and inequitable education made it harder for Black Americans to accrue wealth.

During this period, calls for reparations continued. Ex-slave Callie House of Nashville, Tennessee, launched an ambitious reparations campaign in the 1890s calling on the government to pay pensions to formerly enslaved people.

A 1915 lawsuit against the US Treasury calling for $68 million to be paid to former slaves for unpaid labor was dismissed on the grounds of "sovereign immunity," under which a state is immune from civil action. And political activist Marcus Garvey in the 1920s made reparations central to his Universal Negro Improvement Association movement.

But the debt to Black Americans for the uncompensated labor of their ancestors was not paid. Moreover, the economic outcomes of sanctioned racism under Jim Crow meant that this debt only increased.

The protests and advocacy of the civil rights movement in the 1950s and 1960s bore great fruits, but no reparations.

The Civil Rights Act of 1964 and the Voting Rights Act of 1965 were hard-fought milestones.

But inequities persisted, and, with them, the debt owed. Black and brown bodies were—and still are—disproportionately caught up in the criminal justice system; Black families are less likely to own their own homes; and public education has failed far too many Black youths—all of which has far-reaching ramifications for employment, career success and accumulating wealth. Again, the original unpaid debt has been compounded.

But calls for reparations never went away. In October 1962, the pioneering civil rights activist Queen Mother Moore helped draft a "Resolution for Reparations" that was promoted in the US and around the world.

The organization N'COBRA has, since the 1980s, been campaigning for reparations. More recently there has been author Ta-Nehisi Coates' 2014 article "The Case for Reparations" and calls from groups such as the National African American Reparations Commission along with some Black church leaders. There has been some success on a local level, but no action on a federal one.

Not Too Late

Another campaign for reparations has been successful—the one for the Japanese American citizens interned during World War II.

After the bombing of Pearl Harbor in 1941, President Franklin Delano Roosevelt sent tens of thousands of Japanese Americans to internment camps. In the years after the war, advocates, including the children and descendants of those interred, launched a lengthy campaign, ending with President Ronald Reagan's making a formal apology and signing 1988's Civil Liberties Act, through which each survivor was paid $20,000 each, around $44,000 in today's money.

The campaign for reparations for people of African descent could proceed similarly: a bill, a formal apology and compensation, which could include measures aside from just payment checks—such as education and housing funds, or reforms in the criminal justice system.

The renewed focus on reparations comes at a pivotal time in recent US history. Long considered, rightly or wrongly, as a beacon of democracy and freedom, the US has in the past four years presented a different face to the world amid a retreat into "America first" policy.

Meanwhile, the recent attack on the Capitol, the killing of George Floyd at the hands of police and racial disparities highlighted in the pandemic have raised concerns about the fragility of American democracy and have put the lasting legacies of structural racism in the US on full display.

Paying reparations to Americans of African descent could, I believe, help the US reclaim some moral leadership on the global stage. The US is not the only country in the world with human rights abuses then or now, but it can be one of the few countries in the world that truly addresses these wrongs.

In other words, the US can lead by example.

There Is a Moral Obligation to Reparations

Carissa Véliz

Carissa Véliz is a professor of ethics at Oxford University and is the author of Privacy Is Power: Why and How You Should Take Back Control of Your Data.

Consider the following case. Imagine you inherit a fortune from your parents. With that money, you buy a luxurious house and you pay to get a good education, which later allows you to find a job where you earn a decent salary. Many years later, you find out that your parents made their fortune through a very bad act—say, defrauding someone. You also find out that the scammed person and his family lived an underprivileged life from that moment on.

What do you think you would need to do to fulfill your moral obligations?

Here are some possibilities:

1. Nothing. After all, you are not to blame for your parents' moral faults. You have no moral obligations because, even though you benefited from the fraud, you did it unknowingly and innocently.
2. Find the scammed person and give her your house (or the money you get from it after selling it). It is a way of returning at least part of the fortune to its rightful owner. There is no need to return the money you spent on your education because education is not something that can be sold or transferred. If the wronged person has died, your moral obligations died with her.
3. Find the wronged person and give her your house (or the money you get from it after selling it). If the person has died, you should give that money to her descendants, who are the rightful heirs to the stolen fortune. Children of

"Some Thoughts on Reparations," by Carissa Véliz, Practical Ethics, October 1, 2015. Reprinted by permission.

the wronged person are bound to have inherited at least some of the difficulties and pain that resulted from the scam, and they too deserve to have at least some of their fortune returned.

4. Giving your house to the scammed person or her descendants is not enough because that is only one part of the fortune. You would also have to repay the money you spent during your education (adjusting for inflation). If you do not have enough cash, you should give a part of your salary each month to the wronged person or her descendants until you manage to give back all of the money.
5. Returning all of the money to their rightful owners is not enough. In addition, you are required to provide compensation for moral damages—for all the suffering caused and the years in which the family lived precarious lives. You may compensate monetarily and maybe by putting at the service of the wronged person and her descendants your professional skills and time. (Perhaps you are only required to provide compensation provided it does not represent a great sacrifice for you.)

I recently asked this question at a Spanish forum of scholarship holders. To my surprise, most people who answered (admittedly, not that many) chose the last option.

It seems to me that the last option is supererogatory. In order to fulfill his moral duties, the scammer would certainly need to return the fortune and provide compensation for damages, but his descendants should not be burdened with compensating for an action they did not do. Descendants of wrongdoers should not be punished. If they are obligated to return a stolen fortune it is only because the offspring of the scammed person have a stronger claim to that fortune in virtue of it rightfully belonging to their parents.

In other words, it seems to me that the descendant of the wrongdoers bears harms in returning the stolen fortune. He was misled to believe he was the rightful owner of a fortune, and with that money he made himself a life that he has to give up in order to right a wrong he did not do. In this way, he is harmed. The harm that he suffers, however (which, incidentally, was indirectly caused by his parents), is less than the harms suffered by the scammed person and her descendants. The scammed person and her descendants suffer from the damage of having had their property stolen and they suffer from the precariousness that is caused by a lack of resources.

How much should the descendant of the wrongdoer give back to the offspring of the wronged? I suspect it will partly depend on how wealthy is the former and how badly off are the latter. If, through no fault of his own, the descendant of the wrongdoer lost the fortune in some mishap, it would be unfair to demand that he pay up something he did not know was stolen and does not own anymore. If, at the same time and thanks to some unexpected turn, the offspring of the wronged have done very well, it seems to me that they are owed less.

This is a simplified example. Real world scenarios invite many other factors to take into account. For instance, many cases feature grandchildren, great-grandchildren, and beyond. Perhaps moral obligations get diluted with every generation that creates distance between the wrongdoing and the present. (However, it seems to me that a proper argument needs to be offered as to why it makes a moral difference to inherit stolen property as a grandchild rather than as a daughter or son).

Simplified cases such as this one, however, can inform our moral judgments and may have important implications for international relations. A couple of days ago, Jamaica asked Britain to pay billions of pounds in reparations for slavery. One might object that the case discussed is a disanalogy with respect to Jamaica's request because slavery is nothing like a scam. Britons would not be giving anything back to Jamaicans—they would not be returning stolen money. Rather, they would be giving compensation for moral damages, for the harms involved in slavery. I suspect it is a mistake on the part of Jamaica to frame this case as a case of compensation (if that is in fact what they mean by "reparations"). It seems to me that compensation is only owed by the wrongdoer, and not by his descendants.

Furthermore, for the purposes of this case, slavery can be cashed out as a forceful theft. Slaves worked and produced for others without getting anything in return: the fruits of their work were stolen. There were many other abominable harms involved in slavery, of course, but those were not committed by present-day Britons. It is easier to argue that present-day Britons have nonetheless benefitted from inheriting wealth produced by slaves (arguably, they have not benefitted as much from the other harms perpetrated on slaves). Perhaps Jamaicans would do better in claiming that Britain should return what is theirs, rather than asking for reparations.

In any case, in order to (morally) assess Jamaica's claim, some of the variables to think about are the following: How well off Britain is (and how much of that wealth can be attributed to gains from slavery), how badly off Jamaica is (and how much of that poverty can be attributed to slavery), other reparations Britain would have to make to other countries, whether we think it makes a moral difference how many generations have passed since slavery, how to calculate the amount owed, how much of a sacrifice that would mean for Britons, and whether what is owed is a matter of returning money to their rightful owners or compensating for moral damages.

There Is No Legal Case for Reparations

Luke Moffett

Luke Moffett is a lecturer at the School of Law at Queen's University in Belfast, Northern Ireland.

Two major British businesses have said they will make undisclosed payments to black and minority ethnic groups to atone for their past owners' involvement in the transatlantic slave trade. Pub group Greene King and insurance broker Lloyd's of London have both apologised for what they respectively call "inexcusable" actions and "indefensible wrongdoing."

This comes as UN High Commissioner for Human Rights Michelle Bachelet has called on countries to confront their past involvement in colonialism and slavery to make reparations for those still affected. It also follows the University of Glasgow's announcement last year of a £20 million fund to make amends for benefiting from the transatlantic slave trade.

So what is the legal position when it comes to slavery reparations and where is corporate liability likely to go from here?

The Legal Case

Reparations for slavery have been demanded for centuries for African American, British Caribbean and Caribbean peoples. In 2001, the UN Durban World Conference against Racism recommended reparations for racism, but the momentum was lost as these debates were quickly overtaken by 9/11 and the war on terror.

Since then, research has uncovered numerous individuals and companies that have benefited from slavery in the past. Besides Greene King and Lloyd's of London, the UK banks HSBC, Barclays

"Slavery Reparations: There's Little Legal Basis to Make Companies Pay for Historic Actions," by Luke Moffett, The Conversation, June 19, 2020, https://theconversation.com/slavery-reparations-theres-little-legal-basis-to-make-companies-pay-for-historic-actions-141081.

and Royal Bank of Scotland are all known to have had similar links. In the US the list has included JP Morgan, Bank of America and the clothing retailer Brooks Brothers.

None have paid reparations, although, for example, JP Morgan set up a scholarship fund and apologised for the involvement of its predecessor companies in slavery in 2005. A legal case seeking reparations from the bank and other insurance companies then collapsed in 2006. The payments by Greene King and Lloyd's of London are not reparations in the legal sense either.

In the past few decades, reparations have become a key part of international law in ensuring an effective remedy for those who suffer violations. Reparations are intended to vindicate victims' rights, to reaffirm their dignity as human beings, and to reproach those responsible for their wrongdoing.

Reparations are not so much about money—though money can certainly give victims new opportunities—as confronting those responsible with their wrongdoing and getting them to recognise the value of their victims as human beings.

In the past two decades, there have been increasing reparations paid by corporations for their involvement in historic violations. These have mainly concerned the Holocaust, such as the French and Dutch train operators that transported Jews to concentration camps, Swiss banks that withheld Jewish accounts, and various German corporations, including Bayer and Volkswagen, that benefited from forced labour during the second world war.

Yet these successful cases occurred when survivors were still alive or there was sufficient evidence to find a responsible actor to make reparations. Time makes legal claims go stale. All the victims of the transatlantic slave trade are now long dead, so it is difficult to legally speak of a direct victim who would have standing to bring a claim. Unless new evidence emerges clearly implicating a corporation for it historically profiting from slavery, it is unlikely there will be a basis for a legal case to proceed.

There have been more general reparation claims under domestic law for colonialism, such as the Mau Mau settlement from the British government in 2013, and this year a case which resulted in compensation being awarded in Holland for the killing of Indonesian civilians under Dutch colonial rule.

But these claims were against states, which are more permanent entities than corporations and have different international legal obligations. The 2011 UN Guiding Principles on Business and Human Rights speak of corporations "respecting" human rights by avoiding infringing them and to "address adverse human rights impacts." States, on the other hand, have clear obligations to offer reparations in such situations.

Yet if the legal claim against corporations is quite weak, many may still be seen as morally or politically obliged to consider making amends.

What Reparations Require

Reparations can be framed in other ways if legal avenues are closed. The Caribbean Community (CARICOM) has for years been calling for collective and moral reparations from the European former colonial powers for the continuing harm felt by its 15 member states from the transatlantic slave trade, colonialism and indigenous genocide.

The group's ten-point plan focuses on collective measures in the form of an apology, repatriations to Africa, educational and research opportunities to rebuild cultural institutions, psychological rehabilitation, and debt cancellation. However, no European power has made any efforts to meet the demands—including the UK, which refuses to apologise.

At the same time, the "reparations" announced by Lloyd's and Greene King do not perfectly correspond to victim-centred reparations as understood under international human rights law. There is a risk that just paying money and apologising for past wrongdoing can absolve oneself from the past. Such payments risk being seen as a self-serving public-relations exercise rather than a genuine attempt to atone and prevent the wrongs from happening again.

Instead, a key legal requirement of international reparations is to ensure that the victims participate, so that compensation can be as effective as possible and not simply charity. This is also to avoid replicating power dynamics of benefactor and beneficiary, so that the victims are treated as rights-holders with agency.

How far can such claims making over the past go? Perhaps in dealing with slavery and its pervading effects today we need to revisit the 2001 Durban conference findings. This would involve having a broader conversation about the continuing consequences of historical injustice, and how we can identify and remedy the continuing effects.

Reparations cannot provide a complete solution. No amount of money, memorial or apology can fully remedy the past. Nonetheless, they are a way of acknowledging wrongdoing and victimhood, while seeking justice and social transformation so that such violations do not recur.

Reparations Are Unaffordable and Ethically Disastrous

Graham Hillard

Graham Hillard teaches English and creative writing at Trevecca Nazarene University, a private Christian college in Nashville.

Reparations are an ethical disaster. Proceeding from a doctrine of collective guilt, they are the penalty for slavery and Jim Crow, sins of which few living Americans stand accused. An offense against common sense as well as morality, reparations would take from Bubba and give to Barack, never mind if the former is an insolvent methamphetamine addict or the latter a dweller in near-pharaonic splendor. That reparations are a hopeless cause, supported by only a quarter of Americans, makes them more of an affront to reason rather than less, for it illustrates the enthusiasm with which Democratic politicians will bang their heads against the wall in an attempt to purchase votes.

Even in pragmatic terms, reparations fail. As Michael Tanner argued on NRO last month, the real-world difficulties that would attend such payments "are obvious enough to suggest that the sudden support for reparations amounts to little more than pandering." These difficulties are so extraordinarily compelling that one wonders how the call for reparations retains any support at all. Since the money used to pay for them would have to be raised alongside "the taxes needed to finance [Democrats'] grandiose spending plans," reparations would "totally wreck the economy," sentencing Americans of all races to a future of "higher unemployment, slower wage growth, and less entrepreneurship." Because potential awardees would have to prove their eligibility in some manner, reparations would "be an invitation to perpetual litigation" and would subject America to the spectacle of

"The Other Case Against Reparations," by Graham Hillard, *National Review*, July 22, 2019. Reprinted by permission.

government officials deciding who counts as black. (Rachel Dolezal, your moment has come.)

These are powerful objections, and the case against reparations could easily prevail on their strength alone. Yet they are not the only flaws in the reparations scheme and are, in fact, subordinate to a more fundamental blemish. Even if the practical defects of the project could be overcome, reparations simply wouldn't work. They would not make atonement. They would neither settle nor soothe. In short, they would fulfill none of the promises explicit in the language of their proponents.

Like all political ideas unburdened by their likelihood of actually happening, reparations are frequently spoken of in outlandish terms. In 2018's oft-cited inequality tome *The Divide*, for example, anthropologist Jason Hickel obliterated all previous estimates by placing America's debt to the descendants of slaves at a mind-boggling $97 trillion—about five years' worth of the entire country's economic output—a figure achieved by applying the US minimum wage to every hour of forced labor performed between the years 1619 and 1865. Sensing enemies to her left, presidential hopeful Elizabeth Warren has argued that Native Americans and same-sex couples ought to be given money, as well. That such one-upmanship is a regular feature of a political culture that rewards rallying the base is no surprise. What is surprising—or should be—is the extent to which recent Democratic remarks about reparations have been allowed, with no scrutiny whatsoever, to take on a cast of quasi-religious utopianism.

What are these remarks? They are Kamala Harris's assertion, to NPR, that reparations are an opportunity "to correct course." They are Beto O'Rourke's claim, in his recent and deeply narcissistic Medium post, that reparations are among the "necessary steps to repair the damage done." They are Julian Castro's argument, at South by Southwest, that we are "never going to fully heal as a country . . . until we've addressed"—with reparations—"the tremendous wrong that was done with slavery." Correct course, repair, heal. What such words have in common is their promise that "a national reckoning [can] lead to spiritual renewal." (The phrase is Ta-Nehisi Coates's, but the sentiment belongs to all reparations-mongers.) Pay what you owe, such language suggests, and America can have its soul back. Confess your sin with a large enough check, and you can be forgiven. The problem, as any Christian knows, is that forgiveness only matters if it's permanent. "As far as the east is from the west," the psalmist writes, "so far does God remove our transgressions from us." That assurance, properly understood, is life-changing. And because Christ's redemptive work is finished, God can rightly grant it.

Can the reparations lobby?

To believe that it can, one has to believe that the political apparatus currently pursuing reparations would simply cease to exist upon their being awarded. That no further expiation of the nation's sins would be necessary. For the Left, however, reparations are merely the icing on the existing cake of admissions preferences, minority-contracting requirements, and an eternally expanding welfare state. Ask a progressive if the $97 trillion would make unnecessary any further gestures in the direction of affirmative action, and he will laugh nervously and pretend not to understand the question. If you're lucky, that is. These days, he might very well call forth a Twitter mob to smite you.

The reality is that reparations, however generous, would have nothing like the effect promised by those calling for them. Pay them to African-Americans today, and you will soon be called upon to pay them to others. (In this, if in nothing else, Elizabeth Warren is ahead of the curve.) Compensate one generation, and you will confirm your debt to the next. Reparations will not mend us, restore us, or bring us together. They will only divide, embitter, and impoverish.

We can't afford to pay them. We can't even come close to it. But even if we could, we shouldn't.

Reparations May Be a Moral Imperative, but They Are Also a Political Disaster

Francis Wilkinson

Francis Wilkinson is a former communications consultant who now writes about politics for Bloomberg, among others.

Reparations for black Americans are essential and implausible—a moral imperative inextricably tied to a political disaster.

The disjunction has made reparations a rather contentious topic over the past 150 years or so. The forces of morality seeking compensation for lives and labor stolen from slaves, and which continued to be stolen from slaves' descendants long after slavery officially ended, have never matched the political power of a white majority that collectively prefers to retain the gains of slavery and segregation, however unevenly shared, under the theory that it all happened in a distant, hazy past about which white people don't really want to be reminded anyway.

Nothing about our present politics—racialized, polarized, dysfunctional—suggests the issue will become easier to grapple with anytime soon.

Yet here come the Democrats. Presidential candidates and Senators Cory Booker, Kamala Harris and Elizabeth Warren have in recent weeks all discussed policies that might be loosely associated with "reparations."

In February, House Speaker Nancy Pelosi said she supports establishing a commission to study and consider reparations for slavery. At this month's South by Southwest Festival in Austin, Texas, former San Antonio Mayor Julian Castro, another announced presidential candidate, said, "I've long believed the country should consider reparations because of the atrocity of slavery."

"Reparations: A Moral Imperative and Political Disaster," by Francis Wilkinson, *Seattle Times*, March 20, 2019. Reprinted by permission.

It's hard to believe even this vague talk would be happening without Ta-Nehisi Coates, whose powerful 2014 essay in the *Atlantic* demanded, and won, a new hearing for reparations. Coates is a writer, representing a constituency of one. Unlike politicians running for president, he'll bear no electoral burden for brilliantly reigniting this debate.

The politicians might, however. And given the need of candidates to differentiate themselves in a crowded Democratic presidential field, a single candidate could opt to make a signature proposal of reparations, thereby making life uneasy for the whole party.

If there is a compelling rebuttal to the moral argument for reparations I've not heard it. When police and prosecutors fudge evidence to railroad someone into jail, we expect the victim to be compensated with money drawn from our communal tax dollars. It's unclear why the state-sanctioned exploitation of black Americans over four centuries, which produced gobs of wealth for others, should exist in a different moral universe, one that presumably bends away from justice.

Of course, if morality and justice dictated the course of US politics, President Donald Trump could not be elected to a town council. While we're on the topic, just imagine what a man who transformed a decade of plummeting illegal immigration into "build-the-wall" hysteria could do with a political gift like reparations; it's a demagogue's dream.

Yet Coates' essay may contain a way out of the political threat, as well as a way in. Very little of his essay actually concerned slavery. In fact, Coates devoted most of it not to the "atrocity of slavery" but to the more recent, and more geographically dispersed, racial atrocities of the 20th century.

Crimes of commission—lynching, government-instigated segregation, voter suppression, redlining, employment discrimination—were juxtaposed with crimes of omission, including the modern US history of excluding blacks from those federal government programs that built the white middle class.

Whites gained financial security through Social Security and a broad range of support included in the G.I. Bill and federally backed mortgages for (white) homeownership. Blacks were blocked at every access point, in part because enacting such programs depended on the votes of segregationists who insisted that blacks must remain an impoverished, powerless, lower caste in the nation's apartheid system.

A national discussion of this more recent history—as opposed to cataloging the brutality and wealth extraction of slavery—would still be tricky terrain for Democrats. But it would potentially pay dividends.

Historical knowledge is not Americans' strong suit. Schools generally do a poor job teaching about slavery and the struggle for civil rights. It's an awkward topic, especially in a classroom of racially diverse teenagers. The temptation to speed past the ugliest parts and wallow in bromides is strong.

But a debate—along with a fact-finding commission, as former Representative John Conyers long called for—that focuses on more recent ills would have the ancillary benefit of explaining to Americans exactly how the world's most prosperous middle class was created in the mid-20th century. It was not through the benevolence of conservative "job creators." Federal programs to promote higher education, entrepreneurship and homeownership played important roles then—and can again.

Exploring ways in which blacks were denied access to government programs that elevated whites into the middle class is likely to produce both a more valuable public education and better Democratic politics. White voters in the 21st century are highly unlikely ever to assume responsibility for moral crimes committed by (some of) their ancestors in the 19th century or even the 20th century. Immigrant voters, too, may well balk at paying reparations for brutality that predates their family's arrival on US soil.

But a discussion—even one reduced to clear historical bullet points—of how blacks were excluded from the creation of the middle class would inform discussion about black opportunity and obstacles, while also opening a path to discuss how government promoted the general welfare, with exceptions, in the recent past and how it can do so more equitably in the future. That's a discussion Democrats should welcome regardless of their stands on reparations.

Coates expressed disdain for precisely this sort of morally compromised, politically motivated mini-measure. Acknowledging systematic brutality and exclusion from opportunity is nothing like providing recompense for having long inflicted them in the first place. A commission, for the purpose of education, falls far short of compensation, for the purpose of redress. Meantime, blacks continue to suffer the consequences of longstanding injustice while still being expected to extol the national myth that everyone gets an equal shot (and woe unto the black man who kneels in defiance of it).

As Coates put it, "in America there is a strange and powerful belief that if you stab a black person 10 times, the bleeding stops and the healing begins the moment the assailant drops the knife."

Yet if the stabbing metaphor is apt, there remains a nagging question of when, if ever, the knife was withdrawn and dropped. It certainly wasn't when the Civil War concluded in 1865. Let's begin the investigation there. Then move on to what government and society can do to heal the vicious wounds.

Chapter 2

Would Reparations Have a Positive Economic Impact?

Overview: There Are Many Ways of Building Wealth

Raina Zhao

Raina Zhao is an economics student at the University of California, Berkeley.

During every Congress that has convened since 1989, H.R. 40 has been introduced to the House of Representatives, but it has never even been debated on the House floor. Originally sponsored by Representative John Conyers, H.R. 40 is a bill about reparations for descendants of African American slaves. H.R. 40 does not delineate any material policy to implement reparations. Rather, the bill only moves to establish a federal commission investigating the history of slavery and possible remedies. Even so, it has never been successful.

Unlike in years past, however, public support for reparations has increased, and a historic congressional hearing on June 19th of this year to discuss H.R. 40 received significant media and public attention. Now, prominent Congress members like Bernie Sanders, Elizabeth Warren, Cory Booker, and Kamala Harris have all shown support for the bill. As some of the above Congress members running for president in the 2020 election, such as Harris and Warren, have also floated possible reparations programs in their platforms, the likelihood of legislative action is greater than ever.

The Legacy of Slavery and Racial Wealth Gap

The need for some measures to address the Black-White wealth gap is clear. Past research on the topic indicates the current state of economic inequality across racial lines is shocking: the Federal Reserve found that the median Black household has ten times less wealth than the median white household. Currently, Black

"The Economics of Reparations," by Raina Zhao, *Berkeley Economic Review*, October 11, 2019. Reprinted by permission.

Americans hold less than 2% of the nation's wealth, despite being 12-13% of the US population.

Several factors have contributed to these disparities, but most, if not all, are traced back to the devastating effects of slavery. When emancipation after the Civil War occurred in 1865, General Sherman famously promised reparations in the form of "40 acres and a mule" for every freed slave, but such a program never came to fruition. Instead, in the century and a half since then, former slaves and their descendants have faced unjust compensation in sharecropping, exclusion from owning property through discriminatory mortgage practices, redlining, and employment discrimination.

Black wealth did accumulate in some areas of the nation, like the Greenwood neighborhood in Tulsa, Oklahoma. Greenwood was predominantly African American, and home to a number of wealthy Black-owned businesses like that of O.W. Gurley, a landowner who sold land exclusively to Black buyers, and J. B. Stratford, a hotelier. Greenwood became increasingly affluent, as the number of Black business-owners, attorneys, and bankers grew, and became known as the "Black Wall Street." Most of the money in Greenwood was circulated around the neighborhood itself, rather than being spent outside on white businesses. Greenwood's success soon drew the attention of the white residents living in the surrounding areas. From May 31st to June 1st, 1921, a mob of around 1,500 armed whites, some given weapons by city officials, rioted in the neighborhood. They looted property, burning more than 1,256 homes and leaving more than 8,000 formerly wealthy residents homeless. The Tulsa Riot Race Massacre illustrated how barriers to financial success continued to exist for Black Americans even after accruing wealth.

For many Black descendants of slaves, it has been extraordinarily difficult to amass wealth like their white counterparts. Inequitable economic prospects continue to plague Black Americans even generations after the first emancipated slaves. Low wealth at the onset results in little generational transfer of wealth, with the average Black inheritance being 35% of the value of the average white inheritance. As young Black Americans graduate college, their wealth actually declines on average, as they are more likely than white college graduates to support their parents financially. These factors, among many others, perpetuate the cycle of wealth disparity that started at slavery.

The question now is whether reparations would feasibly and effectively remedy these institutional inequalities, and on whom the onus falls upon to pay for the policy.

What Would Reparations Look Like?

Currently, there is no consensus on the details of a reparations plan. Most of the Democratic Presidential candidates, barring Marianne Williamson, do not advocate for direct payments of cash. In fact, Professor William Darity, an economist at Duke University who has been one of the foremost academics advocating for reparations, found that a lump sum payment could actually increase the relative income of non-Black producers as Black Americans gain more purchasing power and consume non-Black goods, leading to an absolute decline in Black income as a whole. Darity has stressed the importance of programs fostering longevity in financial prosperity, such as a public trust fund giving out grants for asset acquisition like homeownership or higher education.

Another suggestion, championed by Democratic presidential candidate Cory Booker, is a baby bond, or savings issued to every infant at birth (Booker proposes a universal bond, not restricted to Black Americans, making his platform less of a purely reparations policy). Such a bond could be liquidated once the child reaches adulthood, when it could be used for college costs or other expensive endeavors.

Considering how racial income inequality is the primary driver of racial wealth inequality, programs like subsidized higher education to encourage higher incomes for Black Americans may have a significant positive impact on the wealth gap. However, others have argued that government benefits locked for specific purposes are overly paternalistic. An increase in the disposable income of Black Americans would allow for better quality of life as it opens access to higher quality everyday goods, such as healthier food and better healthcare. The freedom to spend a lump sum would also arguably afford more personal dignity to descendants of slaves who have already faced excessive institutional injustices.

With reparations programs, however, also comes the question of how to define their recipients. Professor Darity has argued that reparations should only be restricted to the descendants of slaves, a proposal heartily endorsed by grassroots organizations like American Descendants of Slavery. However, information about ancestry is still not universally ready to be tracked. Furthermore, Pan-African activists have objected to the exclusion of other Black Americans. Activist Nkechi Taifa stated to the *Washington Post*, "It's extremely difficult to separate classes of black people … the idea that unless you can actually trace your family directly to a slave that you haven't been subject to the legacy of slavery is a bunch of hogwash."

The population of Black immigrants to the United States has risen, comprising 8.7% of the Black population. Many Black immigrants come from the Caribbean, which also has a history of slavery. Quantifying reparations recipients will significantly impact how much the government must spend in total to fund such benefits, which brings us to the most ready and vocal argument in opposition to reparations. Who will pay for such an expensive policy?

Costs and Payers

Experts have a wide range of estimates for the exact amount owed to descendants of slaves. Thomas Craemer from the University of Connecticut, for example, placed the total amount at $5.9-14.2 trillion (in 2009 dollars), while Jason Hickel argued that unpaid slave labor from 1619-1865 equaled up to $97 trillion total.

Regardless, with the US federal budget being $4.1 trillion in 2018 ($1.3 trillion of which is discretionary spending), there needs to be a viable way to pay for a robust reparations program. Lawyer

Willie E. Gary argued in favor of suing white Southern families who historically benefitted from slavery, while others have suggested a tax on all households in the top 1% of wealth. Unsurprisingly, these proposals are likely to meet with backlash, especially from Americans who have not historically participated in slavery and feel they should not be penalized for a sin they did not commit. Other methods include government bonds to raise revenue, which may phase out the costs of reparations with future returns to the payer.

Despite the punitive aspects of these proposals, however, the American economy as a whole stands to gain from abolishing the racial wealth gap. The racial wealth gap makes for substantial losses in the national GDP as Black Americans consume and invest far less than they would contribute to the economy if they had a larger share of the nation's wealth. McKinsey reported that the racial wealth gap will cost the US economy between $1 trillion to $1.5 trillion between 2019 and 2028; in other words, closing the racial wealth gap could increase the projected GDP in 2028 by 4-6%.

While the costs and gains of reparations mean that everyone in the United States is a stakeholder, reparations remains a moral issue singularly centered on the experiences of African Americans. The United States cannot reconcile with such an ugly history of racial oppression and brutality without fully addressing it, particularly when such a history still pervades multiple aspects of modern American society. As author Chuck Collins argued to CNN, "People say, 'slavery was so long ago' or 'my family didn't own slaves.' But the key thing to understand is that … the legacy of slavery … created uncompensated wealth for … white society as a whole. Immigrants with European heritage directly and indirectly benefited from this system of white supremacy. The past is very much in the present." With the attention on reparations increasing in both the political and public sphere, the question of recompense for slavery, and more broadly, racial justice as a whole, is here to stay until a satisfactory answer is found.

Industrial Policy Will Truly Address the Legacy of Slavery

Samuel Hammond

Samuel Hammond is the director of poverty and welfare policy at the Niskanen Center. His commentary has been published in the Atlantic, *the* National Review, *and the* American Conservative. *He has also been featured in* New York Magazine, *the* Wall Street Journal, *the* Washington Post, *Vox, and Slate.*

Reparations are now a consensus position within the 2020 Democratic primary.

Let that sink in. From the central plank of Rev. Jesse Jackson's presidential platform in 1984 and 1988, to Ta-Nehisi Coates's blockbuster *Atlantic* essay in 2014—reparations for the descendants of slavery have gone from fringe to mainstream in roughly a generation. What Bernie Sanders called "divisive" only a few short years ago now even finds support among thoughtful conservatives like David Brooks and Michael Brendan Dougherty.

Yet behind the moral clarity of reparations is immense disagreement about what form it ought to take. Should reparations be direct cash payments or land grants? Does a race-neutral "Baby Bond" or refundable tax credit count if white families also benefit? Most Democratic primary candidates have kicked the can to an independent commission. "I support that we should study it," in the words of Kamala Harris. While that may be smart politics, a backlash is already brewing among activists who insist reparations should be, by definition, directed to American descendants of slavery *only*.

Before going down that path, we should think carefully about what a program of direct cash payments to the descendants of slavery

"The Hamiltonian Approach to Reparations," by Samuel Hammond, Niskanen Center, April 29, 2019, https://www.niskanencenter.org/hamiltonian-approach-to-reparations/.

would signify. After all, an act of reparation is distinct from an act of restitution or compensation. Reparations fall into the category of *transitional justice*—one part economic, one part symbolic redress for human rights violations that kicks-off a "reparative" process of truth and reconciliation. They are therefore as much about publicly confronting an injustice as repairing some discrete, calculable harm. A direct payment, in contrast, risks trivializing slavery as merely an issue of "unjust transfer and acquisition," as if the stolen fruits of African American labor neatly correspond to an accounts payable hidden deep within the US Treasury.

Slavery was an act of theft, to be sure. But even more so, it was an act of colonization—one that retarded the development of a population and entire region for generations after emancipation. To truly address that intergenerational legacy, struggling African American communities need investments in infrastructure and a strategy for developing a high-wage workforce. In other words, they need *industrial policy*.

Social Capital and Economic Development

Whites who lost substantial wealth during Reconstruction bounced back within a generation or two. The reason? Despite suffering a large, uncompensated loss, they had existing social capital (their alma mater, a rich relative, a political connection) that opened doors to new opportunities. The same cannot be said for the black communities that experienced depressed economic mobility throughout the sharecropping and Jim Crow eras—and well into the present.

This deficit in economic mobility is what reparations ought to target. Unfortunately, unlike cash, social capital is not so easy to redistribute. Take the fact that half of the 124 most affluent majority-African American neighborhoods are in Maryland. The historical density of federal employment opportunities in the DMV served to integrate black families into middle- and upper-class networks in a way that reproduced across generations. The model worked, but it's not clear how it can be scaled.

Ending restrictive zoning and land-use regulations within major US cities would have an enormous impact on opening social networks, as well, given the role homeownership plays in wealth accumulation and access to quality public schools. Yet we shouldn't fool ourselves into thinking stronger Fair Lending rules or a down-payment subsidy will suffice. To avoid gentrification, urban development in poor neighborhoods must be matched by even more aggressive up-zoning in affluent neighborhoods, dissipating the high rents and property values that lock-in their social capital. This, too, would be hard to scale, not least due to political resistance from incumbent homeowners.

The Toll of Deindustrialization

From redlining to the Deep South, the legacy of slavery is ultimately one of arrested economic development. While industrialization in the 19th and 20th centuries contributed to rising wages for workers in the Northeast and Midwest, Southern lawmakers leaned into King Cotton, committing black workers to the sort of labor-intensive exports we typically associate with developing countries. The mechanization of cotton after 1950 spurred some catch-up growth, but black cotton tenants were largely displaced into similarly low paying service and manufacturing jobs. Catch-up growth slowed in the 1970s, and since 2004 the North-South productivity convergence has stalled.

Today, Mississippi's per-capita income is only 60 percent that of Maryland's, and with more than double the rate of black poverty. Given that one in two African Americans live in the South, and most in the Deep South, the economic legacy of slavery will rollover for as long as that regional productivity gap goes unaddressed.

Research from economists Patrick Bayer and Kerwin Kofi Charles documents how these regional trends have shaped diverging black-white earnings. As they observe, "After narrowing from 1940 to the mid-1970s, the median black-white earning gap has since grown as large as it was in 1950." This is despite strong gains in the top-fifth of black earners, most of whom are college graduates. HBCUs and affirmative action thus appear to have been successful at creating a black upper-class. But left behind—and by some measure *regressing*—are the three-fifths of African Americans with less than a college degree.

While we tend to think of the decline in US manufacturing employment as a white working class problem, it's been even more devastating for African Americans without a post-secondary education. *New York Times* columnist Thomas Edsall explained the dynamic well in his write-up of Bayer and Charles's research:

> Manufacturing jobs started to decline in the late 1970s, preventing black Americans, especially black men, from gaining access to what had been a direct avenue into the middle class for millions of whites before them. At the same time, just as African-Americans achieved voting majorities and political power in major rust belt urban centers during the late 1960s and early 1970s, deindustrialization, the movement of factories to nonunion states, offshoring and, more broadly, globalization ate away at the tax bases of those cities. Newly elected black mayors in cities like Detroit and Cleveland faced diminished resources, eroding their ability to use political power to build a middle class as Irish, Italian and Polish and other ethnic leaders had before them.

Look no further than Flint, Michigan, where industrial flight has devastated its predominantly black working class. Cash-based reparations won't fix this. Infrastructure and human capital investments at least stand a chance.

Toward a National Infrastructure Bank

Following the Great Recession, the Obama Administration proposed creating a "National Infrastructure Bank" to finance public works and other major projects throughout the country. The idea was ultimately sidelined amid the healthcare reform debate, but the legislation could easily be revived. From the Flint water crisis, to the developmental gaps throughout the Deep South, such a bank (or a collection of regional banks) could be tasked with making the kinds of strategic investments that cash-strapped local governments can't and the private sector won't.

A National Infrastructure Bank needs an initial capitalization, but afterward would be self-financing through bonds. It follows the same model used by post-war Germany and the East Asian economies to bootstrap rapid economic development. Germany's development bank, KfW, also played a critical role during East-West reunification, and has since helped sustain the country's advance manufacturing sector.

If this proposal has a Hamiltonian ring to it, it's no accident. Alexander Hamilton proposed a "system of public credit" designed to make "internal improvements" throughout the US at the First Congress in 1790. Hamilton earned his appreciation for economic development policy after spending years working in the West Indies, where the limitations of a plantation economy based on a single agricultural export were self-evident. His conflict of visions with Thomas Jefferson pitted a strong federal industrial policy against agrarian localism, presaging the eventual bifurcation of the North and South.

The US economy has changed enormously since the nation's founding. Nonetheless, reparations are premised on the notion that history has echoes in the present. In economics, the importance of history is called "path dependency," and breaking out of it is the core preoccupation of every successful industrial policy. If Democrats have any sense, it will be the core preoccupation of their reparations agenda, as well.

Black-Led Resistance Movements Are Paving the Way for Reparations

Sarah Freeman-Woolpert

Sarah Freeman-Woolpert is a writer, researcher, and organizer focused on nonviolent social movements and creative action. She lived for two years in the Balkans, studying and supporting youth activist movements. She now works as a grassroots organizer for peace and justice and is based in Boston.

Months after the police killing of George Floyd sparked racial justice protests around the world, Black Lives Matter activists are once again flooding the streets—this time in response to the recent police shooting of Jacob Blake in Kenosha, Wisconsin. Among the demands that continue to ring out is the call for reparations, or payment to people of African descent. Several African countries—including Namibia, Burundi and the Democratic Republic of the Congo—have also joined the call, demanding reparations from European countries for the perpetration of genocide under colonialism.

For many US communities, these questions have been the subject of debate and discussion for years. In Ferguson, Missouri, one group of community leaders came together in 2014 after the police killing of Mike Brown to found the Truth-Telling Project—an initiative to share stories, educate communities and drive structural change against racism and systemic violence. During the COVID-19 pandemic, the Truth-Telling Project has been working on a COVID-19 Community Story Project to lift up the stories of how the pandemic has affected the lives of people of color.

Co-founder David Ragland has witnessed the movement for reparations transform over time—from the streets of Ferguson to the recent Congressional victory of Black Lives Matter activist Cori Bush. I spoke with Ragland about the role of resistance in the fight for reparations, and the changing landscape of racial justice organizing at this historic moment.

You worked closely with Cori Bush in founding the Truth-Telling Project. What does her victory over William Lacy Clay in St. Louis signify for the role of movement leaders to shift political power in the United States?

Cori is bringing the movement to Washington, D.C., to explain why people go to the streets. Clay represented the class strivings of the baby boomers, who often sought to become a part of the system without challenging it enough. Our parents wanted us to be a part of the system so we could have a better life. Cori's vision demands a better life, while also demanding economic, social, ecological and political justice.

I believe that hope is emerging to challenge the issues that our generation is grappling with, like climate change, racial justice and gender identity. We also see the global issues that connect the injustice here with injustice abroad.

You have written about the "Four Rs" of reparations: resistance, repentance, restitution and reconciliation. What is the role of resistance specifically in the movement for reparations?

This moment of resistance is opening the door to things people wouldn't even consider just six months ago. When the protests began around the country, people thought, "Oh, these are new ideas." But to some extent they're just new to the larger American public.

In South Africa, you wouldn't have had Truth and Reconciliation without resistance to bring attention to what was happening. But as we resist, our resistance has to be able to educate. Some civil rights–era policies like affirmative action benefit more white women than Black people, and the Fair Housing Act is currently part of the legislation fueling gentrification in urban communities for the last three decades, if not more. If we create a reparations program, for example, we have to make sure that racist banks are not benefitting [from that program]. So resistance is part of the continuum of making people aware with truth-telling.

As co-founder of the Truth-Telling Project, what are some of the things that have changed in the context of Black Lives Matter organizing since the shooting of Mike Brown in Ferguson?

Truth-telling really came along as a way to reinforce some of the experiences that were coming out of Ferguson, as well as places like Baltimore and Minneapolis, where Freddie Gray and Phillando Castille were murdered. We had people from around the country come to share stories, and we created an online curriculum called "It's Time to Listen." We partnered in solidarity with a number of groups, including Indigenous folks and Latinx folks, to add voices telling stories and shifting narratives.

[The Truth-Telling Project has] always been rooted in this truth and reconciliation framework, asking ourselves what kind of process can help our society get from where it is to where it needs to be. Over time, the hearings helped us see that stories weren't enough—that we needed reparations.

Indigenous land and Black bodies fueled [American capitalism]. They were the first inputs, they're the people who maintained it and made this country possible. If you go to any major city in the United States and look at a building or structure, some person of color helped to create it. They didn't get credit for it, and they were underpaid and abused while doing it. If many churches in Maine were built [on the profits of] mercenaries who sold the scalps of Indigenous people for $1,000 each, reconciliation is over. Reconcile with what? Pay reparations. Give back land. Restore sovereignty. It's that simple for me. It's a debt and it has to be paid.

If we ever want to get to reconciliation, you have to set it right. That's gonna have a cost, and it shouldn't just be on the government. Reparations have to be from both white institutions and white individuals, whether their relatives benefited from slavery or not.

This society is irredeemable unless it pays the bill for what it's done. I was a little bit more hopeful that peoples' stories would change the way people behaved, that we would be able to connect on an empathetic level, and that people would be able to feel the pain we were experiencing and want to change. Then I realized the only God in this country is money. So that's where we're at.

I wonder if you could speak more about the role of faith communities and religious institutions in paying reparations. Archbishop Desmond Tutu played such an important role in the truth and reconciliation process in South Africa, and you've written about the role of faith communities in the history of slavery and oppression. Why is the role of religious institutions so important?

Religion was one of the core methods used to maintain slavery. Churches operated as slush funds for slaveholders who essentially brought wealth into these institutions. In 1805, the Anglican Church created what they called the Slave Bible. They removed all passages about liberation and freedom and justice from it, and they promoted it around the Caribbean and southern states where slavery was happening.

So there is a long legacy of faith communities not just selling slaves and owning slaves, but propagating the institution of slavery, benefiting from discrimination and reinforcing neighborhoods' segregation codes. Martin Luther King Jr. famously said that Sunday was the most segregated day in America.

When it comes to reparations—if not churches, if not mosques, if not temples, then who? God's justice has to begin somewhere, and it begins with God's people. So it is an urgent moral and spiritual responsibility that I believe is connected with the salvation of not just individual white folks, but with the entire nation.

You have also written about enacting reparations through measures like a gentrification tax, or looking at income and land to create a land trust that benefits people historically impacted

by violence. What are some of the other policies that movements are advocating to be part of a national reparations process?

[What we need are ways for] people to redistribute wealth, allowing them to begin making what we call interpersonal repair. But reparations are rooted in what the communities need, not what people want to do. This also entails measures like defunding the police, for which there is urgent importance, especially if you think about police as descendants of slave catchers and the way they operate in our communities. Defunding the police would contribute to mental health and community [well-being] because people have so much fear of how police deal with certain situations.

We can shift to think more about the role of social workers and educators in our communities, while acknowledging that both of those fields also need to be decolonized. We need a Black parent-to-teacher pipeline, because most new teachers are likely white, and most new white teachers go to Black neighborhoods without a background in restorative justice. I don't know if I want those people teaching my kid.

Then we have the food supply, and the importance of supporting community gardens and garden-shares. We need legislation so people can grow their own food locally in their communities.

But this reparations process is going to look different in different communities. In St. Louis, churches and universities owe a great deal. Washington University has completely gentrified University City, where Black people lived and hung out. So it's real. It is putting the truth at these peoples' feet and asking them to respond to it. There are various policies like ending the military transfer of weapons to local police departments, cutting support for the Pentagon, ending weapons manufacturing—it all has to be on the table now. That's what makes this moment so important, and that's why we can't stop now.

Voluntary Reparations Should Be Supported by Everyone

Theodore Kalambokidis

Theodore Kalambokidis works in economic consulting and has written articles for fee.org.

As they do every year, the House of Representatives is currently considering HR 40, the "Commission to Study and Develop Reparation Proposals for African-Americans Act." If this commission is ever created, it should consider voluntary reparations as an easy first step.

Voluntary reparations should be supported by everyone regardless of their opinions about involuntary reparations. (For the record, I think former slaves should have been paid reparations after the Civil War, and black people who lived through and suffered under Jim Crow should be financially compensated today. I'm not sure how much they are owed or who should pay.)

What Are Voluntary Reparations?

For simplicity, let's assume reparations mean a cash payment to some group of beneficiaries. The beneficiary group could be all African-Americans, only descendants of slaves, people who were alive during Jim Crow, or some other subset. The reparations would be paid for by some subset of people separate from the beneficiary group. Most proposals call for involuntary reparations, meaning that if you are in the chosen group, you are compelled by law to pay.

In contrast, under a system of voluntary reparations, anybody could choose whether or not to fund the reparations payments. If you choose to pay any amount, your money would be transferred to somebody in the beneficiary group. Your payment would be

"The Case for Voluntary Reparations," by Theodore Kalambokidis, Foundation for Economic Education, July 7, 2019, https://fee.org/articles/the-case-for-voluntary-reparations.

recorded. If a future law were passed compelling payment of reparations, you would be exempt from paying (at least up to the amount you already paid).

Similarly, if you were in the group of beneficiaries, you might choose to not receive reparations. (In testimony before Congress, author Coleman Hughes argued that he and the one-third of black Americans who do not support reparations should not be forced into victimhood. With the voluntary receipt of reparations, this would not be a problem.)

Voluntary Reparations Should Be Uncontroversial

Everybody should support voluntary reparations, no matter their opinion on involuntary reparations. The only people who would be affected by reparations would be those paying for or receiving them.

Payers and receivers might or might not support involuntary reparations. Let's consider four groups of people:

1. those receiving reparations who support involuntary reparations;
2. receiving but oppose involuntary reparations;
3. paying and support;
4. paying and oppose.

Let's entertain a hypothetical policy where a system of voluntary reparations is enacted.

How might it affect each group?

1. If you are in the receiving group and support involuntary reparations, there is no reason to oppose voluntary reparations. At worst, nobody will volunteer payment, and nothing will have changed. At best, everybody will volunteer to pay you and everybody else in the receiving group full reparations. With anything short of full volunteer payment, you can continue pushing for involuntary payment. Voluntary reparations in no way preclude involuntary reparations.

2. You may oppose reparations either because you don't want to receive them or you don't think people should have to pay them. Under a system of voluntary reparations, paying and receiving are both optional.
3. You may choose to pay whatever amount you think is right. The beneficiaries will receive some reparations. Even if full reparations are never achieved, your payment will still do some good. Again, voluntary reparations in no way preclude involuntary reparations.
4. You don't have to pay. What do you care if other people choose to spend their own money on reparations?

The Voluntary Model Is Applicable to Some Other Government Spending Decisions

Voluntary reparations are somewhat analogous to the charitable contribution tax deduction. You would be free to donate to a charity and deduct the amount from your taxable income, thus reducing the amount you paid for all government programs. With voluntary reparations, you would be free to pay reparations and reduce the amount you had to pay for a specific government program, i.e., theoretical future involuntary reparations. Unlike the charitable tax deduction, voluntary reparations would decrease your tax liability by the same amount as your voluntary contribution if and only if involuntary reparations became law.

Some people already donate to organizations like the NAACP and the Southern Poverty Law Center, which do reparations-type work. Allowing contributions to private reparations-like organizations to generate a credit against future involuntary reparations payments could be a feasible adaptation of the charitable tax deduction.

The simple voluntary model is only applicable to cases where each marginal dollar is useful, even if the full ideal amount is never achieved. Direct transfers to people, like income-support and reparations payments, have this property. Contrast this with a government project like building a bridge. If the bridge costs at least $X to be built, all the money contributed will not be useful unless the full amount is achieved. Half a bridge is not half as useful as a full bridge. Half an income support check is half as useful as the full check.

For cases where the funding is only useful if the full amount is achieved, more sophisticated voluntary payments could still work. For example, Kickstarter funds private products by making voluntary payments conditional on achieving the full funding amount. If the funding threshold is not reached, no payments are made. An excludable (to avoid the free rider problem) bridge or football stadium could theoretically be funded by voluntary taxes along the lines of Kickstarter. People would vote with their dollars as to whether a government project is worth pursuing.

For now, let's start with the easy case of voluntary reparations.

Cash Reparations Won't Work

Corey Walker

Corey Walker is from Chicago and has a background in economics, history, and technology.

In 2014, Ta-Nehisi Coates's famous "The Case for Reparations" essay ignited a public debate on whether the descendants of slavery and Jim Crow deserve cash payouts. This topic came to the forefront of the national conversation again during the past summer's explosive protests following the death of George Floyd. There's no doubt that America's legacy of racial oppression had a significant impact on the economic condition of Black Americans. Most liberals would agree that government policy should addresses historical discrimination and racial disparities. However, reparations in the form of a cash payment remain a deeply unpopular idea that likely would not produce their intended effects.

Reparations Are Politically Infeasible

From 1989 to 2017, Representative John Conyers of Michigan annually submitted H.R. 40, a bill that provides funding for the study of reparations programs for the descendants of American slavery. The bill has failed to make it out of committee even once. However, candidates in the 2020 Democratic primary overwhelmingly supported H.R. 40 when they discovered its use as an answer for the pesky "reparations" question that wouldn't enrage the invaluable black base or alienate racially resentful white voters necessary to win a general election.

During the height of the George Floyd protests, Reuters/Ipsos conducted a poll that found only one in five Americans supported reparatory payments for African Americans. Unsurprisingly, nearly 80% of Republicans were opposed to it and only one-in-

Corey Walker, "Would Reparations Work?" *Exponents Magazine*, February 12, 2021.

three Democrats supported it. Only one in ten whites supported reparations payments. However, perhaps the most surprising stat the poll found is that only around half of Black Americans supported reparations. During the largest protest movement in American history, completely centered on racial justice, support for reparations remained extremely unpopular among white people and divisive among Blacks.

Looking at these polls, it becomes easy to understand why Democratic politicians are very wary of answering questions about reparations in a straightforward manner. Since Biden's inauguration, we haven't heard much about reparations or H.R. 40. This is for a good reason. Reparations continue to be unpopular and politically toxic.

Large Cash Transfers Often Don't Have Lasting Success

Proponents of reparations argue that direct payouts to descendants of slavery would close the stubborn economic gaps that still remain between blacks and whites. Though tempting to believe, there's not much evidence that it would work out this way.

There are different reparations schemes out there, but most involve lump sum payments. Ta-Nehisi Coates advocates for lump sum payments. The *New York Times*' Jamelle Bouie supports a "baby bonds" program in which Black Americans are given a low-yield government savings account that can be cashed in at 18 years old.

Reparations beneficiaries could be compared to lottery winners in that both are the recipients of a lump sum of cash. Lottery winners typically receive larger amounts of cash than what reparations recipients would receive, showing that even massive cash-infusions typically don't permanently lift a person's economic fortunes. We have substantial data that shows lottery winners often go bankrupt. In fact, a Florida survey showed that lottery winners were twice as likely to go bankrupt than non-winners.

The Georgia Land Lottery of 1832 distributed highly valuable parcels of land randomly. One would expect that the descendants of these individuals would be the wealthiest families in Georgia. However, that isn't the case.

A paper by economists Hoyt Bleakley and Joseph Ferrie tracked the descendants of these land lottery winners and discovered they had no better outcomes in wealth or education than the descendants of others. Bleakley theorizes that this can be partially attributed to the lack of human capital development. These fortunate families did not send their children to schools at higher rates, therefore suggesting a lack of investment in education.

What Can We Do?

So what can the government do to help heal the economic wounds created by America's history of racial oppression?

Building off of Bleakley and Ferrie's research, building human capital within the Black community can lead to long term and sustainable economic growth and stability.

Attacking these educational gaps should start as early as possible. To combat the black-white educational gap, America could institute universal Pre-K. These programs would be a boon for the poor and research suggests it would reduce the achievement gap for Black and low-income children. Black students are far less likely to attend high schools with advanced math and science curriculums and AP courses. Changing zoning laws to allow more for more affordable housing in traditionally affluent areas would grant Black families better access to quality public schools.

Free community colleges and Historically Black Colleges and Universities would help young Black people climb the economic ladder. Around a quarter of community college students are Black, and community college students are more likely to be low income and first-generation on average. Likewise, HBCUs educate a large swath of the Black professional class. HBCUs produced 80 percent of Black judges, 40 percent of Black lawyers, 40 percent of Black engineers, and 12.5 percent of Black CEOs. Formulating a plan that would specifically target HBCUs would likely prove very difficult. However, an alternative could be to give any college a $5,000 grant per-student in exchange for dropping tuition. Under this plan, 41 HBCUs would be able to drop their tuition to zero and not lose money.

Criminal justice reform would also go a long way in building social capital within Black communities. Far too many Black men are in prison. Despite making up only 6 percent of the population, Black men account for 50 percent of prisoners. There's a case that Black boys, in particular, are more likely to act out and achieve lower educational attainment without their fathers in their lives.

There are many ways for the government to help address racial disparities. However, the focus on reparations misses the mark entirely. Reparations are politically poisonous and would not likely close the black-white economic gap. There are better ways to redress America's legacy of racial discrimination.

Reparations Won't Solve America's Race Problem

Stefan Spath

Stefan Spath was formerly executive director of the Foundation for Economic Education.

There has been much debate recently about reparations for slavery. According to its proponents, the federal government should award Americans of African descent financial damages solely because slavery, as an institution, existed in the United States from the founding until almost a century later.

Three principal arguments are offered: (1) The legacy of slavery has hindered the economic progress of blacks in America; (2) reparations would serve as a damage award that would rectify a historical wrong committed by the United States; and (3) reparations would give poor blacks more disposable income, which would increase their living standards and lift entire black communities.

On the surface, these arguments seem to have a modicum of legitimacy. However, because of the potential divisiveness that the issue is sure to have, it is important to closely examine the premise on which these arguments are based. To do that effectively, we must first look at the institution of slavery itself from a historical perspective.

Slavery as an institution existed on every inhabited continent of the earth for at least 4,000 years of recorded history.

Slavery was a truly global phenomenon: Europeans enslaved other Europeans; Asians enslaved other Asians; Africans enslaved other Africans; and Native Americans enslaved other Native Americans. In fact, the origin of the word "slavery" itself comes from Slav, as in the Slavic people of eastern Europe and the

"What's Wrong with Reparations for Slavery?" by Stefan Spath, Foundation for Economic Education, June 30, 2010, https://fee.org/articles/whats-wrong-with-reparations-for-slavery/.

Balkans. During the middle ages and throughout the early stages of the Ottoman Empire, Slavic villages in what is modern-day Yugoslavia (Serbia) and Croatia were regularly raided by Barbary pirates, Arab slave traders, and Ottoman conquerors in search of men, women, and children to enslave. During the eighteenth century it wasn't uncommon for up to half the slaves for sale on the island of Zanzibar, an Arab colony off the east coast of Africa, to be Caucasian. In short, people of all races, not just blacks, have been enslaved, and virtually every culture in the world has a grievance.

The only thing unique about slavery in the West is that it was abolished here. One of the earliest anti-slavery documents was Pope Pius II's 1462 condemnation of slavery as a "great crime." British abolitionists, who for the most part were evangelical Christians, championed the legislative revolution that brought about manumission in Britain and her colonies.

In the West, once the abolitionist momentum was underway, there was no turning back. This was especially the case in the United States, where the ideological underpinnings of a constitutional republic made it increasingly difficult rationally to deny slaves their rights. The abolition of slavery in the United States marked a historically significant moral high point, not only for this country, but also for the entire world. By the end of the nineteenth century, slavery as an institution was non-existent in the West and only existed in small pockets of Africa, Asia, and the Middle East.

Has Slavery Hindered the Economic Progress of Blacks?

Economist Thomas Sowell, in his seminal work *Civil Rights: Rhetoric or Reality*, concluded after exhaustive statistical research that the vast majority of whites and blacks believe there are a higher percentage of blacks in poverty than there actually are. Indeed, when surveyed, most whites and blacks believe three-quarters of black Americans live below the official poverty line, when in reality only one in four do, according to the 2001 Census.

Why is there so much confusion? Part of the problem is the perception that "black" and "poor" are synonymous. In the 1960s it was politically expedient to associate the state of being poor, uneducated, and oppressed with being black. The civil rights establishment found this association rhetorically necessary to focus public attention on the plight of southern blacks and to engage the emotions of the white majority against overt southern racism.

However, this political strategy had an unexpected impact on the emerging black middle class. According to the black-equals-poor logic, when the black middle class achieved more opportunity and became more educated and affluent, it essentially became less "black." This perhaps explains the black establishment's attitude toward Supreme Court Justice Clarence Thomas and national security adviser Condoleezza Rice. Essentially, black identity was hijacked and frozen during the 1960s.

Unfortunately, the image of poverty stricken blacks in need of government handouts to get by is still perpetuated by race demagogues like Jesse Jackson and Al Sharpton, who stand to gain politically by fostering that stereotype. It is a truism of politics that charlatans in search of political power will always benefit from having a constituency with a chip on its shoulder.

Is there a legacy from slavery that has hindered the economic progress of blacks today? Let's consider the numbers. Major marketers have long constructed a black "gross national product" (GNP) from government statistics to gauge the financial power of black Americans. This is actually a misnomer since it tries to measure the total products and services consumed, not produced, by the black community. This statistic is often cited by black political leaders to persuade corporate America to produce more goods suited to the preferences of blacks. It turns out that if black Americans constituted their own country, they would have the 11th largest economy in the world.

In addition to being a wealthy demographic group (richer than 90 percent of the people in the world), blacks in America have a longer life expectancy than African and Caribbean blacks, as well as whites in many parts of Eastern Europe and Latin America. Black Americans have higher rates of literacy and achieve more postsecondary degrees as a percentage of the population than blacks in Africa. Black Americans' upward mobility from Reconstruction to the present is a testament to their creativity and ability to adapt. Reparations are not only unnecessary as a financial corrective, but they would also be an insult to the multitudes of successful black Americans who lifted themselves out of poverty before and after the civil rights movement.

Who Gets What?

If the proponents of reparations take to the courts, it will be interesting to see their principle for determining who is entitled to what. For many reasons that will be a Herculean task.

Because of centuries of migration, conquests, and intermixing, racial purity is more of a social construct than a biological fact. Intermarriage between whites and blacks in America over the past two centuries has produced a large population of individuals who defy the stark dichotomy.

Racially mixed populations in other parts of the world, such as in Latin America, have created classifications to describe themselves based on racial portions as small as an eighth. However, the practice of racial classification has evolved differently in the United States.

In an effort to deny inheritance rights to illegitimate progeny born by slave women, racist plantation owners in the antebellum South created the dreaded "one-drop rule" to discourage the courts from calling their miscegenational offspring anything but Negro. The nomenclature of this racist practice has survived to this day and is embraced by both blacks and whites, who for the most part are unaware of its discriminatory beginnings. Consider how Vanessa Williams and Colin Powell are labeled black despite their interracial heritage.

With so much racial intermixture, will those who dole out the potential reparations demand certificates of racial purity? The thought is preposterous. Another quagmire in paying reparations is that a small percentage of blacks were free before slavery ended, having bought their freedom or having had it bequeathed to them by sympathetic slave owners. Are their descendants eligible for reparations?

In antebellum New Orleans it wasn't uncommon for freemen of color to own slaves. That blacks owned slaves has been a hotly debated point. It is true that a vast majority of blacks who bought slaves did so to emancipate relatives and friends. However, there are several well-documented cases of black slave owners in Louisiana who kept their slaves in servitude for life.

Black slave ownership poses a serious conundrum in the equitable distribution of reparations. Few Americans, white or black, are familiar enough with their genealogies to know, with any certainty, significant details about what their ancestors were doing almost two centuries ago.

Then there is the case of African and Caribbean émigrés from the post-Civil War era. It is estimated that this subgroup of the black community comprises between 3 to 5 percent of the total black population in the United States. Will they pay or receive reparations?

More Reparations?

In some respects one could argue that reparations for slavery have already been paid. These implicit reparations, the argument goes, have taken the form of direct monetary transfers such as welfare payments or nonmonetary benefits such as hiring and admission quotas. Indeed, policies based on racial preferences such as affirmative action have allowed hundreds of thousands of blacks to enter universities and obtain employment based on criteria different from those applied to other groups of people.

It should not be overlooked that the greatest irony of American slavery is that the descendants of those brought across the Atlantic from Africa are demonstrably better off than the descendants of those who remained. Sub-Saharan Africa is home to some of the poorest countries with some of the most appalling living conditions in the world. Disease, war, and famine are commonplace, and corrupt governments led by military dictators and kleptocrats ensure that economic growth and development for the masses is a low priority. In his book *Out of America: A Black Man Confronts Africa*, American reporter Keith Richburg concludes that black Americans should consider themselves lucky to have escaped the squalor of what is contemporary Africa.

Not only blacks, but all Americans should feel lucky to be born in the society with the most opportunities for advancement. The American dream is not a myth but a reality—so attractive that tens of thousands of people from across the world try to make it to our shores every year. The benefits of living in the United States weaken, if not destroy, the foundation of the argument in favor of paying blacks group compensation for what happened to their ancestors.

In a system where politicians steal from Peter to pay Paul, the politicians, as George Bernard Shaw once pointed out, can always count on the support of Paul. But does this redistribution of wealth leave anyone better off? Yes. The people who receive the hard-earned money confiscated from the taxpayers will undoubtedly be materially better off. However, to judge whether such a policy is sound, one must look beyond the immediate effect and try to discern the impact on other groups.

In that respect, reparations would not be an economic stimulus because wealth would merely be shifted from its producer to someone else—no new wealth would be created. Applying the wisdom of Frédéric Bastiat in looking for what is unseen in public policy, we could say that the economic benefits of reparations are countered by the taxpayers' invisible opportunities compulsorily forgone. Put in this context, how could one argue that the expenditure of reparations by blacks would be an economic stimulus?

An economist as such cannot make normative judgments about a policy and remain true to his discipline. He cannot tell us how to correct the historical crime of slavery (assuming it can be corrected at this late date). What economics can teach us is that if policymakers appropriate the wealth of one group to pay reparations to a second group because a third (dead) group did nasty things to a fourth (dead) group 150 years ago, it would create a plethora of problems. Chief among them would be racial animosity and the festering of a truly debilitating mentality of "victimization" among black youths.

Are Current Taxpayers Culpable?

Of the three primary arguments for reparations, the argument for damages is the most irrational. Though slavery was widespread in the southern United States, slave ownership was not. It is estimated that less than 10 percent of whites owned slaves. The vast majority did not; they had neither financial nor agricultural resources to warrant slave labor. Slave ownership was restricted to a highly concentrated group of wealthy southern elites—the landed aristocracy.

Today we live in a country with a population of 285 million people. Because of immigration, it is safe to argue that the majority of white people in this country are descended from post-Civil War immigrants who had nothing to do with slavery.

Many ethnic groups that arrived on American shores in the early twentieth century, including the Irish, European Jews, and Chinese, were subject to severe discrimination. However, with every passing generation, ethnic groups developed the occupational skills, knowledge, and cultural norms necessary to fully assimilate and rise to higher socioeconomic levels within the mainstream American culture.

Why, then, should the descendants of these groups, let alone first-generation Americans, be financially liable to blacks as a group? In the American legal system, damages hinge on the principle of cause and effect—one pays for the damage one causes. In the case of slavery, there is no culpable person alive to pay for the crime.

Perhaps the most important error made by those who argue for reparations is not economic at all but philosophical. The idea of achieving justice by taking money from one group to pay another for an act that was neither committed nor suffered by the parties is a collectivist affront to the American ideal of individualism. People are not interchangeable pawns but individuals responsible for their own actions. Slaves and slave owners are dead, and we cannot bring them back.

Our Constitution provided the framework for legal equality for all individuals, and later legislation eliminated remaining race-based government barriers to freedom, assuring that blacks, like whites, can be beneficiaries of this great system. Thus the only solution to the race problem in America is a commitment to individualism.

Cash Payments Hurt Those Who Receive Them

Robert Rector and Mimi Teixeira

Robert Rector is a researcher at the Heritage Foundation. Mimi Teixeira is a legislative director at the US House of Representatives.

The idea behind universal basic income (UBI) policy has a record of failure. Policymakers seeking to reform the welfare state should focus on policies proven to work. Appropriate priorities for welfare reform are (1) insisting on budgeting transparency about the full costs of the 89 federal means-tested programs providing cash, food, housing, medical assistance, and other social services to poor and low-income Americans; (2) promoting work; and (3) removing penalties in the welfare state that discourage marriage. UBI policies expand the welfare state and undermine work.

Universal basic income (UBI), also referred to as guaranteed minimum income, is a social welfare policy that provides cash payments to all citizens. A variant provides cash aid to all individuals but phases out aid at some income level. Recent advocates include libertarian scholar Charles Murray,[1] former union leader Andy Stern,[2] and innovators Elon Musk[3] and Mark Zuckerberg.[4] The mayor of Stockton, California,[5] recently announced his intent to launch such a program.[6]

The premise of universal basic income has a known track record of failure that hurts recipients and increases dependence on government, based on test experiments on the closely related negative income tax policy.[7] In four controlled random assignment experiments[8] across six states between 1968 and 1980, the comparable policy was shown to reduce yearly hours worked among recipients significantly.[9] For each $1,000 in added benefits, there

"Universal Basic Income Harms Recipients and Increases Dependence on Government," by Robert Rector and Mimi Teixeira, The Heritage Foundation, February 14, 2018. Reprinted by permission.

was an average $660 reduction in earnings, meaning that $3,000 in government benefits was required for a net increase of $1,000 in family income.[10] The results of these studies led policymakers to shift their focus to work-based welfare benefit programs.

Additional Flaws in Comprehensive UBI Policy

Additionally, a comprehensive UBI policy would:

- **Transfer funds away from the vulnerable to affluent persons capable of self-support.** A comprehensive UBI policy directs money to those who do not need it, including relatively affluent families and young adults without dependents.
- **Eliminate Social Security and Medicare payments and transfer funds to able-bodied non-working adults.** Virtually all policies advocating a guaranteed minimum income eliminate Social Security and Medicare payments. Such a policy shifts resources from the elderly to non-elderly, able-bodied adults without dependents. This poorly targeted welfare makes the policy an inefficient use of financial resources.
- **Increase government spending and the scope of government.** Current government policy makes a distinction between the elderly and disabled who cannot work to support themselves and able-bodied non-elderly adults who can and should work to support themselves. Aid to the latter group is conditioned largely on work; assistance is given only when individuals are in need, and able-bodied recipients are expected to work or prepare for work as a condition of receiving aid. In principle, work-capable adults who refuse to work or prepare for work do not receive aid. The UBI eliminates all distinctions between the elderly, disabled, and work-capable adults. Able-bodied adults who refuse to work are entitled to the same benefits as everyone else. By establishing a new universal entitlement and by creating for the first time a moral expectation that able-bodied adults who refuse to support themselves should be entitled to aid from the taxpayer, a UBI would set the stage for a massive expansion of government.

- **Reduce work and increase recipient dependence.** The overwhelming majority of Americans believe that able-bodied adults should be required to work or prepare for work as a condition of receiving aid.[11] This was the core principle behind welfare reform in the 1990s. As noted, the UBI abandons that principle. By removing work requirements from welfare, UBI would decrease work among the poor and increase dependence on government.
- **Increase pressure for greater redistribution to eliminate income inequality.** By reducing the complex variables of the current welfare state to a single variable of what level of support the guaranteed income will provide, this proposal would put greater pressure on politicians to increase redistribution.
- **Misdirect attention to the administration of the welfare state rather than the effect of programs on work and marriage.** Administrative costs are the wrong target for reform because they are not the reason for the high cost of the welfare state. For the most part, administrative costs in welfare are only 10 percent of total costs.[12] Therefore, simplifying administration cannot result in substantial savings. The real problem in welfare is not administrative costs but an incentive structure that reduces work[13] and marriage.[14]

Conclusion

Universal basic income policy is an idea with a record of failure; policymakers seeking to reform the welfare state should focus instead on policies proven to work.

Appropriate priorities for welfare reform are (1) insisting on budgeting transparency about the full costs of the 89 federal means-tested programs providing cash, food, housing, medical assistance, and other social services to poor and low-income Americans;[15](2) promoting work;[16] and (3) removing penalties in the welfare state that discourage marriage.[17] UBI policies would undermine work and expand the welfare state.

Endnotes

1. Charles Murray, "A Guaranteed Income for Every American," *The Wall Street Journal*, June 3, 2016, https://www.wsj.com/articles/a-guaranteed-income-for-every-american-1464969586 (accessed February 6, 2018).
2. Robert Kuttner, "A Conversation with Andy Stern on the Case for a Universal Basic Income," *The American Prospect Longform*, June 28, 2016, http://prospect.org/article/conversation-andy-stern-case-universal-basic-income (accessed February 6, 2018).
3. Chris Weller, "Elon Musk Doubles Down on Universal Basic Income: 'It's Going to Be Necessary,'" *Business Insider*, February 13, 2017, http://www.businessinsider.com/elon-musk-universal-basic-income-2017-2 (accessed February 6, 2018).
4. Todd Haselton, "Mark Zuckerberg Joins Silicon Valley Bigwigs in Calling for Government to Give Everybody Free Money," CNBC, May 25, 2017, https://www.cnbc.com/2017/05/25/mark-zuckerberg-calls-for-universal-basic-income-at-harvard-speech.html (accessed February 6, 2018).
5. Alix Langone, "This US City Will Give Its Poorest People $500 a Month—No Strings Attached," *Time*, January 24, 2018, http://time.com/money/5114349/universal-basic-income-stockton/ (accessed February 12, 2018).
6. The Economic Security Project, an advocacy group for universal basic income policies, will provide the initial funding for the program. The final goal of the Economic Security Project is to have UBI policies funded through government. Note also that the initial experiment will provide the cash payments only to a sample of low-income residents, while the idea for a permanent UBI policy includes payments to most or all citizens. Stockton Economic Empowerment Demonstration, "How Will SEED Be Funded?" October 10 2017, https://www.stocktondemonstration.org/faqs/who-is-funding-this (accessed February 13, 2018); Economic Security Project, "Who We Are," https://economicsecurityproject.org/who-we-are/ (accessed February 13, 2018).
7. The negative income tax is a policy idea similar to the idea of a universal basic income. In a negative income tax system, everyone is guaranteed a minimum income that is phased out as earnings increase. For the purposes of evaluating work disincentives through these experiments, the difference between the two policies is not relevant. The experiments showed that the major reduction in employment was not due to the phaseout of benefits. SRI International, *Final Report on the Seattle–Denver Income Maintenance Experiment, Volume 1, Design and Results*, May 1983, pp. 127–128.
8. See note 5, supra.
9. Gary Burtless, "The Work Response to a Guaranteed Income: A Survey of Experimental Evidence," in Alicia H. Munnell, ed., *Lessons from the Income Maintenance Experiments*, Proceedings of a Conference Held in September 1986, sponsored by the Federal Reserve Bank of Boston and the Brookings Institution, Federal Reserve Bank of Boston Conference Series No. 30, 1986,

p. 26, https://www.bostonfed.org/-/media/Documents/conference/30/conf30b.pdf (accessed February 8, 2018).

10. Ibid., p. 28.

11. According to an online survey conducted by The Heritage Foundation, 92 percent of respondents support work requirements for able-bodied adults to receive government benefits. Elizabeth Fender, "Poll: Vast Majority Support Four Simple Fixes to Welfare System," Heritage Foundation *Report*, December 7, 2017, https://www.heritage.org/public-opinion/report/poll-vast-majority-support-four-simple-fixes-welfare-system.

12. Robert Rector and Rachel Sheffield, "Five Myths About Welfare and Child Poverty," Heritage Foundation *Backgrounder* No. 3176, December 20, 2016, https://www.heritage.org/welfare/report/five-myths-about-welfare-and-child-poverty.

13 Robert Rector and Vijay Menon, "Obama Gutted Work Requirements for Welfare. Why Trump Is Right to Restore Them," Heritage Foundation *Commentary*, August 31, 2017, https://www.heritage.org/welfare/commentary/obama-gutted-work-requirements-welfare-why-trump-right-restore-them.

14. Robert Rector, "How Welfare Undermines Marriage and What to Do About It," Heritage Foundation *Issue Brief* No. 4302, November 17, 2014, https://www.heritage.org/welfare/report/how-welfare-undermines-marriage-and-what-do-about-it.

15. Robert Rector, "Examining the Means-tested Welfare State: 79 Programs and $927 Billion in Annual Spending," testimony before Committee on the Budget, US House of Representatives, May 3, 2012, https://www.heritage.org/testimony/examining-the-means-tested-welfare-state-79-programs-and-927-billion-annual-spending.

16. Robert Rector and Rachel Sheffield, "Setting Priorities for Welfare Reform," Heritage Foundation *Issue Brief* No. 4520, February 24, 2016, https://www.heritage.org/welfare/report/setting-priorities-welfare-reform.

17. Robert Rector, "Reforming the Earned Income Tax Credit and Additional Child Tax Credit to End Waste, Fraud, and Abuse and Strengthen Marriage," Heritage Foundation *Backgrounder* No. 3162, November 16, 2016, https://www.heritage.org/welfare/report/reforming-the-earned-income-tax-credit-and-additional-child-tax-credit-end-waste.

Chapter 3

Have Reparations Succeeded in the Past?

Overview: Reparations Worked Before—Just the Other Way Around

Thomas Craemer

Thomas Craemer teaches public policy at the University of Connecticut.

The cost of slavery and its legacy of systemic racism to generations of Black Americans has been clear over the past year—seen in both the racial disparities of the pandemic and widespread protests over police brutality.

Yet whenever calls for reparations are made—as they are again now—opponents counter that it would be unfair to saddle a debt on those not personally responsible. In the words of then-Senate Majority Leader Mitch McConnell, speaking on Juneteenth—the day Black Americans celebrate as marking emancipation—in 2019, "I don't think reparations for something that happened 150 years ago for whom none of us currently living are responsible is a good idea."

As a professor of public policy who has studied reparations, I acknowledge that the figures involved are large—I conservatively estimate the losses from unpaid wages and lost inheritances to Black descendants of the enslaved at around US$20 trillion in 2021 dollars.

But what often gets forgotten by those who oppose reparations is that payouts for slavery have been made before—numerous times, in fact. And few at the time complained that it was unfair to saddle generations of people with a debt for which they were not personally responsible.

There is an important caveat in these cases of reparations though: The payments went to former slave owners and their descendants, not the enslaved or their legal heirs.

"There Was a Time Reparations Were Actually Paid Out—Just Not to Formerly Enslaved People," by Thomas Craemer, The Conversation, February 26, 2021, https://theconversation.com/there-was-a-time-reparations-were-actually-paid-out-just-not-to-formerly-enslaved-people-152522.

Extorting Haiti

A prominent example is the so-called "Haitian Independence Debt" that saddled revolutionary Haiti with reparation payments to former slave owners in France.

Haiti declared independence from France in 1804, but the former colonial power refused to acknowledge the fact for another 20 years. Then in 1825, King Charles X decreed that he would recognize independence, but at a cost. The price tag would be 150 million francs—more than 10 years of the Haitian government's entire revenue. The money, the French said, was needed to compensate former slave owners for the loss of what was deemed their property.

By 1883, Haiti had paid off some 90 million francs in reparations. But to finance such huge payments, Haiti had to borrow 166 million francs with the French banks Ternaux Grandolpe et Cie and Lafitte Rothschild Lapanonze. Loan interests and fees added to the overall sum owed to France.

The payments ran for a total of 122 years from 1825 to 1947, with the money going to more than 7,900 former slave owners and their descendants in France. By the time the payments ended, none of the originally enslaved or enslavers were still alive.

British "Reparations"

French slave owners weren't the only ones to receive payment for lost revenue, their British counterparts did too—but this time from their own government.

The British government paid reparations totaling £20 million (equivalent to some £300 billion in 2018) to slave owners when it abolished slavery in 1833. Banking magnates Nathan Mayer Rothschild and his brother-in-law Moses Montefiore arranged for a loan to the government of $15 million to cover the vast sum—which represented almost half of the U.K. goverent's annual expenditure.

The U.K. serviced those loans for 182 years from 1833 to 2015. The authors of the British reparations program saddled many generations of British people with a reparations debt for which they were not personally responsible.

Paying for Freedom

In the United States, reparations to slave owners in Washington, D.C., were paid at the height of the Civil War. On April 16, 1862, President Abraham Lincoln signed the "Act for the Release of certain Persons held to Service or Labor within the District of Columbia" into law.

It gave former slave owners $300 per enslaved person set free. More than 3,100 enslaved people saw their freedom paid for in this way, for a total cost in excess of $930,000—almost $25 million in today's money.

In contrast, the formerly enslaved received nothing if they decided to stay in the United States. The act provided for an emigration incentive of $100—around $2,683 in 2021 dollars—if the former enslaved agreed to permanently leave the United States.

Similar examples of reparations going to individual slave owners can be found in the records of countries including Denmark, the Netherlands and Sweden, as well as Argentina, Colombia, Paraguay, Venezuela, Peru and Brazil.

The French government even set an example on how the government can conduct genealogical research to determine eligible recipients. It compiled a massive six-volume compendium in 1828, listing some 7,900 original slave owners in Saint Domingue and their French descendants.

Reparations, This Time the Other Way Round …

Blessed with detailed US Census records and local archives, I believe the government could do the same for the Black descendants of enslaved Americans.

In the 1860 census, the last one before the Civil War, the government counted 3,853,760 enslaved people in the United States. Their direct descendants live among close to 50 million Black residents in the United States today.

Using historic census records to estimate the number of man-, woman-, and child-hours available to slave owners from 1776 to 1860, I estimated how much money the enslaved lost considering the meager wages for unskilled labor at the time, which ranged from 2 cents in 1790 to 8 cents in 1860. At a very moderate interest rate of 3%, I arrived at an estimate of $20.3 trillion in 2021 dollars for the total losses to Black descendants of enslaved Americans living today.

It is a huge sum—roughly one year's worth of the US's GDP—but a figure that would comfortably close the racial wealth gap. The difference is, in contrast to historical precedents, this time the benefits would go to the Black descendants of the enslaved, not to enslavers and their offspring.

How Reparations Worked Between Germany and Israel

Lily Gardner Feldman

Lily Gardner Feldman teaches at Johns Hopkins University and is the author of Germany's Foreign Policy of Reconciliation: From Enmity to Amity.

The thorny issue of reparations for war-time crimes against humanity, material losses, despoliation, and human rights abuses has dominated the political sphere in the last several months. On the international front, both Greece and Poland have renewed demands for war-related reparations from Germany. At home, the topic of reparations for slavery, Jim Crow, and all manner of discriminatory social policies and practices has featured prominently in the 2020 presidential campaign. In his June 2014 seminal article in the *Atlantic*, "The Case for Reparations," Ta-Nehisi Coates asked whether the September 1952 German-Israeli Reparations Agreement could be instructive for the American debate. The recent anniversary of the Agreement provides us with an opportunity to revisit this question and extend it to international cases. First, we must consider how unusual the agreement was for the two parties. Then we can address the issues of motivation, content, leadership, opposition, and legacy.

Uniqueness

The fact of negotiation and settlement just seven years after the end of the war and the Holocaust was remarkable given the vividness of memory and the depth of physical and psychological wounds on the part of the victims. The chief Israeli negotiator, Felix Shinnar, called the treaty "the most memorable in history." Moshe Sharett,

"The September 1952 Reparations Agreement Between West Germany and Israel: The Beginning of a Remarkable Friendship," by Lily Gardner Feldman, American Institute for Contemporary German Studies. Reprinted by permission.

the Israeli foreign minister at the time, characterized the signing as a "political fact of enormous international significance, something quite unprecedented, which has taken a most momentous place in the history of Israel and of Germany."

For Germany to this day the Reparations Agreement with Israel has remained unique as the Federal Republic has granted formal reparations to no other country. Under the 1953 London Debt Agreement on Germany's pre-war and war-time debts, it was agreed that the issue of reparations would be shelved until there was a formal peace treaty between Germany and victim countries and claimants. Israel was the only exception as the negotiations with the Jewish state on reparations pre-dated the conclusion of the London Debt Agreement. The September 1990 two-plus-four agreement between the two Germanies and the four war-time Allies, which sealed unification, was technically not a peace treaty, rendering reparations legally and politically settled and a non-issue from the German perspective.

When Greece formally asked for reparations and payment of forced loans and debts in June 2019 (informal requests began in 2015 at the height of the Greek debt crisis) to the tune of $330 billion, Germany used the two-plus-four argument to reject the claims. Germany further believes that its provision of some $54 million to Greece in 1960 also settled the issue of compensation whereas Greece insists this comprised mainly (inadequate) payments to individual citizens (mostly Jewish) and not to the state.

The 2015 election of the conservative Law and Justice party in Poland moved the question of reparations to the top of Poland's agenda with Germany. By August 2019, following the work of a parliamentary commission, Germany's reparations debt was assessed at more than $850 billion. Germany insists that the 1990 two-plus-four agreement made reparations moot, and besides Poland gave up its right to claims when it signed the Bierut Treaty with the German Democratic Republic in 1953. Poland retorts that the Soviet Union forced it to conclude the agreement, making it invalid. The head of Poland's parliamentary Committee on Reparations has drawn a direct comparison with payments to Israel and individual Jewish recipients: "[There are still Polish citizens alive] who experienced the same suffering as the Jewish nation [but received nothing from Germany]."

Motivation

What propelled Israel and Germany to negotiate just seven years after the end of the Holocaust and Germany's total defeat? Chancellor Konrad Adenauer's memoirs reveal an important moral imperative for Germany given the fact and nature of its crimes. But Adenauer's thinking was also highly pragmatic: he knew that Germany would not return to the "family of nations" unless it dealt with its horrific past. The United States in particular, in the person of John McCloy first as US Military Governor in Germany and then as US High Commissioner, insisted in July 1949 that Germany be pro-active: "The world will carefully watch the new West German state, and one of the tests by which it will be judged will be its attitude towards the Jews and how it treats them."

In Israel, in 1951 and 1952 moral arguments concerning direct negotiations with Germany could be found among both advocates and opponents. One side argued the moral justice of claims, while opponents contended that there was a moral obligation to refuse any contacts with Germany or Germans. Israeli leaders also employed highly pragmatic reasoning: the fledging Israel economy was on the brink of collapse and there was little financial support coming from the outside world; the only place where economic help could be found was Germany.

Content

The negotiations over reparations and material losses were preceded by a major public statement on the part of Adenauer in the Bundestag on September 27, 1951. It recognized that "unspeakable crimes [against Jews] have been committed in the name of the German people" during the Third Reich and the Holocaust and offered to negotiate with Israel and representatives of world Jewry over compensation. The negotiations were shrouded in secrecy, were conducted in a third country, and the Israeli negotiators, most of whom had a German-speaking background, refused to speak German. The German-Israeli Reparations Agreement of September 1952 was signed in a third city, Luxembourg, and involved neither handshakes nor speech. It was ratified in March 1953.

The Agreement provided Israel over a twelve-year period with 3 billion DM ($7 billion today), as goods in kind rather than cash payment, that built the infrastructure of the Israeli economy. The figure was based on the amount required by Israel to absorb 500,000 refugees (those escaping Nazism before the Holocaust and those who survived the Holocaust). Israel assessed the cost of absorption at $3,000 per immigrant. In addition, the Conference on Jewish Material Claims Against Germany, representing world Jewry, received 450 million DM for disbursement to individuals. Germany also committed itself to pass indemnification and restitution laws to cover individual victims. The Indemnification Law was passed in 1953 and amended in 1965; the Restitution Law was enacted in 1957, with a final amendment in 1969. Forty percent of the recipients of these two pieces of legislation lived in Israel. Germany uses the term "Wiedergutmachung" or "making good" to describe the composite compensation that derived from the 1952 Agreement. Israel instead uses the term "shilumim" suggesting material compensation as Germany can never make up for the "massacre and despoliation" it wrought against Jews.

Leadership

The Agreement would not have been possible without the visionary leadership of Chancellor Konrad Adenauer and Prime Minister David Ben-Gurion. They both embodied the admixture of political interest and moral necessity; they both saw the short-term and long-term implications of the Agreement; they both negotiated the choppy waters of opposition that plagued both sides and acted decisively to combat it. The personal connection they forged after the Reparations Agreement was expressed in an active correspondence between the two leaders.

Opposition

Opposition to the Reparations Agreement was fierce and entrenched in both Germany and Israel. In Germany, the rejection of negotiations was anchored in political and economic interests. A variety of CDU and CSU Bundestag members opposed the negotiation out of concern about Germany's ability to pay for it. In the early 1950s, Germany was still deeply challenged by the structural ravages of war. These members voiced their concern by opposing the 1953 ratification of the Agreement. Politicians like Franz-Josef Strauss and Fritz Schäffer, both CSU deputies (Schäffer was also finance minister), objected to the negotiations and conclusion for fear of a threatened Arab economic boycott and loss of markets in the Middle East. The Deutsche Partei and the FDP objected to the Agreement because of its adverse effects on relations with the Arab world. In the end, the Agreement was ratified by 239 deputies with 35 votes against and 86 abstentions, but Adenauer had to rely on the SPD to secure passage. Opposition to the Agreement was also evident in public opinion polls: In a 1952 survey, 44 percent of Germans deemed the Agreement unnecessary and only 35 percent registered positive response (11 percent unqualified support plus 24 percent support if the amount of reparations were reduced).

The very idea of negotiating with Germany generated violent opposition in Israel, most notably on the occasion of the January 1952 Knesset debate on direct negotiations with the Federal Republic. Orchestrated by the Herut Party under the leadership of Menachem Begin (later Israel's prime minister), there were fierce demonstrations outside the Knesset and clashes with the police; in the end, the army had to quell the riot. The demonstrations outside the Knesset were matched by acrimony within. Begin contended that negotiations would be a "revolting abomination" that would mean taking "blood money" from the perpetrators.

Herut was not alone in opposition. The religious parties, Mapam, the General Zionists, and Maki all resisted the government's plan with the argument that it was immoral to negotiate with Germany. Nonetheless, there was a positive outcome with 60 in favor, 51 against, 5 abstentions, and 4 absentees.

Legacy

The Agreement was the first step on a path leading to reconciliation between Germany and Israel. The way was often strewn with stones. The Agreement led to close economic ties between the two countries for after its end in 1965, Israelis would purchase German machinery and equipment to replace those provided by the Federal Republic. After the ice was broken in 1952, other bilateral "miracles" happened in the 1950s and beyond: the beginning of important relations in science and technology, in defense and intelligence, and in youth exchange. Almost seventy-five years after World War II and the Holocaust, German-Israeli relations are characterized by both countries as a deep "friendship" involving a panoply of bilateral institutions at the governmental and societal levels. However, echoing the situation in the early 1950s, public opinion in Germany is highly critical of Israel, especially its policy toward the Palestinians. Surprisingly, Israeli public opinion overwhelmingly supports relations with Germany, a development that could not have been foreseen when Israel began to negotiate with Germany in 1952.

The US Has Issued Reparations Before

Rhoda E. Howard-Hassmann

Rhoda E. Howard-Hassmann teaches human rights at Wilfrid Laurier University in Canada, and she's the author of, among others, the book Human Rights and the Search for Community.

In June, the United States House of Representatives held a debate about reparations to African-Americans. One of the questions in this discussion is why Japanese-Americans received reparations for their internment by the US federal government during the Second World War, yet African-Americans have yet to receive reparations for their ancestors' enslavement or for other crimes committed against them.

I published an article comparing reparations to Japanese-Americans and African-Americans in the journal *Social Forces* in 2004 after a colleague, Rodney Coates, professor of Global and Intercultural Studies at Miami University, asked me this question.

My explanation is not a moral judgment on whether African-Americans should receive reparations. I believe that they should. My explanation is a scholarly interpretation of the differences between the two movements. These differences explain why it will be more difficult for African-Americans than Japanese-Americans to receive reparations.

Conditions for Reparations

It is much easier to obtain reparations under the following conditions:

- The number of victims is relatively small.
- The victims are easily identifiable.
- Many of the direct victims are still alive.

"Why Japanese-Americans Received Reparations and African-Americans Are Still Waiting," by Rhoda E. Howard-Hassmann, The Conversation, July 17, 2019, https://theconversation.com/why-japanese-americans-received-reparations-and-african-americans-are-still-waiting-119580.

- The injustice took place during a relatively short time period.
- The perpetrator is known.
- The injustice is easily identifiable.
- The injustice offends values of equality, personal safety and/ or the right to own property.
- There is a symbolic victim around whom advocates for reparations can rally.
- The amount of reparations asked for is not so large that the public will find it unreasonable.

The number of Japanese-American victims was relatively small, about 120,000. They were also easily identifiable as people of ethnic Japanese descent, whether citizens or not. The injustice took place between 1942, when the Japanese were first interned, and 1945, when the war ended.

The perpetrator, the US government, was easily identifiable. The internment of Japanese-Americans violated the values of ethnic equality and ownership of property, since their property was confiscated. The Japanese-Americans were not tortured or murdered, however.

Quite a few former internees were still alive in 1988 when reparations were offered. US Senators Daniel Inouye and Spark Matsunaga became symbolic victims. They were both Second World War veterans and Inouye had lost an arm in battle. Finally, the amount paid was relatively low, $20,000 for each of 80,000 living survivors, for a total of about $1.6 billion.

Wider, More Severe Injustices

Compared to Japanese-Americans, enslaved African-Americans and their descendants endured much more severe injustices. Enslavement violated all norms of personal safety; owners were permitted to beat and torture enslaved people, and in some cases even to murder them. The violations offend all our contemporary norms of racial equality.

Enslaved African-Americans were also not permitted to own property and were themselves the legal property of others.

Slavery was abolished in 1865, but many injustices were perpetrated during the post-1865 Jim Crow period and beyond. These included continued violations of bodily safety, such as lynchings and police shootings. Segregation and discrimination violated the principle of equality. And even when African-Americans earn the same incomes as their white contemporaries, they own much less wealth because they do not inherit from generations of property owners.

It is easy to identify the perpetrators of these injustices. But there are so many that it might be difficult to persuade any one perpetrator to pay reparations. At minimum, perpetrators include the US federal government and the governments of every state that ever permitted enslavement of African-Americans. More broadly, they include municipal governments, private businesses, educational institutions and churches.

Social Movements for Reparations

The problems in organizing reparations to African-Americans lies in the other characteristics of successful social movements for reparations. It is difficult to identify which people of African descent in the US today are the descendants of enslaved people.

If all descendants are considered worthy of reparations, regardless of the number of generations since their ancestors were enslaved, then the number might be in the tens of millions.

None of the direct victims of enslavement are still alive. And there is no single individual who can be considered symbolic of the reparations movement, because all the immediate victims are long dead. Perhaps, though, one could be chosen, such as Michelle Obama. Both her grandfathers were grandsons of enslaved people.

Some people who advocate for reparations also ask for such a large amount that the public would probably find it unreasonable. For example, in his 2004 debate with me, Rodney Coates asked for $12-15 trillion, which is 60 to 75 per cent of the US Gross Domestic Product of $20.5 trillion in 2018.

This doesn't mean that it's impossible for the movement for reparations to African-Americans to succeed. A social movement for businesses, universities and churches to acknowledge their roles in slavery and the Jim Crow era has already started. Georgetown University in Washington, for example, has offered reparations in the form of preferential admissions to the 4,000 descendants of the 272 slaves it sold in 1838.

There have also been reparations for some injustices during the Jim Crow period. In 1923, about 120 African-Americans were burned out of their homes in Rosewood, Fla., and several were murdered. In 2002, victims and victims' descendants were awarded $2 million in compensation.

Thus, attaining reparations to African-Americans is not an impossible dream. But it is, and will continue to be, much harder than it was for Japanese-Americans.

Reparations After World War I Failed to a Disastrous Degree

The Historian of the US Department of State

The State Department's Office of the Historian is staffed by historians who deal in the history of US foreign policy and the Department of State.

In the years following the First World War, issues of debt repayment and reparations troubled relations between the Allies and the now defeated Germany. The US-sponsored Dawes and Young Plans offered a possible solution to these challenges.

At the end of the First World War, the victorious European powers demanded that Germany compensate them for the devastation wrought by the four-year conflict, for which they held Germany and its allies responsible. Unable to agree upon the amount that Germany should pay at the Paris Peace Conference in 1919, the United States, the United Kingdom, France, and the other Allies established a Reparation Commission to settle the question. In the spring of 1921, the Commission set the final bill at 132 billion gold marks, approximately $31.5 billion. When Germany defaulted on a payment in January 1923, France and Belgium occupied the Ruhr in an effort to force payment. Instead, they met a government-backed campaign of passive resistance. Inflation in Germany, which had begun to accelerate in 1922, spiraled into hyperinflation. The value of the German currency collapsed; the battle over reparations had reached an impasse.

US Loans to Allied Powers

Meanwhile, a second wartime financial issue was causing tension among the former co-belligerents. While the United States had little interest in collecting reparations from Germany, it was determined

"The Dawes Plan, the Young Plan, German Reparations, and Inter-allied War Debts," Office of the Historian. Reprinted by permission.

to secure repayment of the more than $10 billion it had loaned to the Allies over the course of the war. Time and again, Washington rejected calls to cancel these debts in the name of the common wartime cause; it also resisted efforts to link reparations to inter-allied war debts. In 1922, London made this link explicit in the Balfour Note, which stated that it would seek reparations and wartime debt repayments from its European allies equal to its debt to the United States. That same year, Congress created the United States War Debt Commission to negotiate repayment plans, on concessionary terms, with the 17 countries that had borrowed money from the United States.

The Dawes Plan

In late 1923, with the European powers stalemated over German reparations, the Reparation Commission formed a committee to review the situation. Headed by Charles G. Dawes (Chicago banker, former Director of the Bureau of the Budget, and future Vice President), the committee presented its proposal in April 1924. Under the Dawes Plan, Germany's annual reparation payments would be reduced, increasing over time as its economy improved; the full amount to be paid, however, was left undetermined. Economic policy making in Berlin would be reorganized under foreign supervision and a new currency, the Reichsmark, adopted. France and Belgium would evacuate the Ruhr and foreign banks would loan the German government $200 million to help encourage economic stabilization. US financier J. P. Morgan floated the loan on the US market, which was quickly oversubscribed. Over the next four years, US banks continued to lend Germany enough money to enable it to meet its reparation payments to countries such as France and the United Kingdom. These countries, in turn, used their reparation payments from Germany to service their war debts to the United States. In 1925, Dawes was a co-recipient of the Nobel Peace Prize in recognition of his plan's contribution to the resolution of the crisis over reparations.

The Young Plan

In the autumn of 1928, another committee of experts was formed, this one to devise a final settlement of the German reparations problem. In 1929, the committee, under the chairmanship of Owen D. Young, the head of General Electric and a member of the Dawes committee, proposed a plan that reduced the total amount of reparations demanded of Germany to 121 billion gold marks, almost $29 billion, payable over 58 years. Another loan would be floated in foreign markets, this one totaling $300 million. Foreign supervision of German finances would cease and the last of the occupying troops would leave German soil. The Young Plan also called for the establishment of a Bank for International Settlements, designed to facilitate the payment of reparations.

The advent of the Great Depression doomed the Young Plan from the start. Loans from US banks had helped prop up the German economy until 1928; when these loans dried up, Germany's economy floundered. In 1931, as the world sunk ever deeper into depression, a one-year moratorium on all debt and reparation payments was declared at the behest of President Herbert Hoover; an effort to renew the moratorium the following year failed. At the Lausanne Conference in 1932, European nations agreed to cancel their reparation claims against Germany, save for a final payment. After the November 1932 election of Franklin D. Roosevelt, France and the United Kingdom resurrected the link between reparations and war debts, tying their Lausanne Conference pledge to cancel their claims against Germany to the cancellation of their debts to the United States. The United States would not accept the proposal. By mid-1933, all European debtor nations except Finland had defaulted on their loans from the United States.

Nevertheless, the Dawes and Young Plans were important US efforts that had lasting consequences. Coming so soon after the US rejection of the Treaty of Versailles and the League of Nations, the Dawes and Young Plans were significant instances of

US reengagement with European affairs. The Young Plan also had a more lasting effect: the Bank for International Settlements, or BIS, continues to operate to this day as a forum for central bank consultation and cooperation. The United States' experience with inter-allied war debts continued to influence its foreign policy for years to come; this influence is evident in the Johnson Act in 1934, the Neutrality Acts of the 1930s, and the Lend-Lease program in the Second World War.

South Africa's Reparations Program Has Been a Disappointment

Ashley Ridge

Ashley Ridge is a writer who was involved in the Southern Methodist University partnership project with South African History Online.

After the end of apartheid, the South African government found itself left to tend to not only a scarred nation, but also gaping wounds that had yet to be treated. In order to begin this lengthy healing process, the government formed the Truth and Reconciliation Commission. The task of the Truth and Reconciliation Commission, otherwise abbreviated as the TRC, was to deal with cases of "gross human rights violations" committed during apartheid by seeking out perpetrators and victims and arranging confession hearings, as well as granting amnesty to repentant perpetrators and reparations to deserving survivors. As part of the Truth and Reconciliation Commission's mandate, the government sought to issue reparations to citizens who had suffered "gross human rights violations," but victims and analysts alike criticized the implementation of these standards. Additionally, because of the South Africa's large and diverse population, granting reparations to all victims was already an impossible endeavour from the start.

No matter how many lives are eased, there will always be some remaining tension. Many Africans are still dissatisfied with what they have received from the TRC and the South African government, which begs the question of how effective the TRC's efforts were. While some believe that the government has done its best and now any additional repair is left up to South African citizens, others believe that the TRC failed in properly granting

"The Failure of Good Intentions: What Went Wrong with the Truth and Reconciliation Commission upon Granting Reparations?" by Ashley Ridge, SAHO, December 6, 2012.

reparations. Some believe this failure adds up to the definitions of who deserves reparations being too wide, and that victims were invalidated as a result. Others believe that the government was too soft in handling perpetrators and that these individuals were not properly punished. Yet another set of criticisms describes that the TRC itself was corrupt. However, findings suggest another set of criticism that underlines the fact that there was simply too little in the way of resources to grant retribution-based reparations. Because of these factors, it is logical to conclude that the struggle to acquire adequate reparations for everyone is far from over.

The TRC's Mission

Like most projects, the Truth and Reconciliation Commission started out with good intentions. In their original proposal, the TRC stated that the meaning of these reparations was to "help victims overcome the damage that they suffered, to give them back their dignity and to make sure that these abuses do not happen again" (1995:1.2). In going over the moral basis reparations, the TRC included a bulleted list of their standards:

- Victims of gross human rights abuses have the right to reparation and rehabilitation because of the many different types of losses they have suffered.
- Victims need to be compensated in some way, because the amnesty process means they lose the right to claim damages from perpetrators who are given amnesty.
- The present government has accepted that it must deal with the things the previous government did and that it must therefore take responsibility for reparation. (1995:1.3.1)

In a way, the act of granting reparations served not only as an act of compensation, but as a type of protection for citizens. The TRC realized that part of their protocol, granting amnesty to wrongdoers, would sacrifice the chance for those who have been wronged to finally claim justice; however, claiming justice was not the point of their mission. At the point in time the TRC began its work, such methods of attaining retribution-based reparations were impossible. Perpetrators would be granted amnesty for their actions, making the notion of seeking vengeful justice hypocritical and problematic. If the TRC were to forgive perpetrators, then turn around and subject them to harsh punishment, this would only stir more uproar. While what went on under apartheid is worthy of being addressed, the TRC was under a tight bind; they had to tread lightly in order to solve remaining conflicts as peacefully and simply as possible. A key element identified in the mission statement of the TRC was responsibility, which further underlines the importance of these reparations. Another aspect of the TRC's aim was to take up for what the South African government failed to do in the past. It is undeniable that countless wrongs were committed under apartheid, but the old government either ignored or sanctioned these acts. By granting reparations to victims of the old government, the TRC was finally able to publicly acknowledge the horrors their citizens underwent. In their original proposal, they went thoroughly over the process of granting reparations and all that entailed:

> Consultative workshops were held throughout the country. All the information collected by the Committee helped it to: find out the harm that was suffered; find out what the needs and expectations of victims are; work out ways to identify and help victims in immediate need; and make proposals for long term measures for reparation and rehabilitation. (1995:1.4.1)

Their ultimate goals were to keep these reparations "development-centred; simple, efficient and fair; culturally appropriate; community-based; and promoting healing and reconciliation." (1995:1.4.2) Their list of goals and standards goes on and on, and continue to sound of nothing but good intentions. So what went wrong? Firstly, we will have to examine how this process worked.

How Reparations Worked

The TRC determined who to grant reparations by holding multiple open workshops, where all citizens were allowed to attend and air their grievances. These workshops were held all throughout the country, some taking several days. Each workshop was transcribed accordingly for further evidence. Such a setup provided the TRC with the ability to hear multiple viewpoints and cases at once.

One such hearing took place in Pietersburg. While the purpose of this hearing was to air grievances it highlights several other tensions within South African society that could not be easily mended through reparations. One of the first speakers was a man by the name of Mr. Lategan, who stated:

> Chairperson, I've spent almost all my adult life trying to persuade White people that all the people living in South Africa are citizens of this country and to accept the logical consequences of such a reality. That has brought deep division in the White community especially in this Province. Politics beset every fibre of our community, in our schools, in our Churches, in our agricultural unions, in our cultural organisations, every bit of the community got politicized and polarized. Sir, I never abandoned my own people, I stayed with them helping them through the difficult times of reform firstly because it was my duty and also because I love them. I've never been a broker or an advocate for the Right Wing tendencies yet if my Black friends want to understand the past, they need to understand what the cause of these Right Wing tendencies were.
>
> [...] Sir we have a wonderful country and we have a beautiful Province, we have everything in our favour. We as the people of this Province must learn to work together. Let us purge our hearts of all the bitterness of differences of the past. A wound must be cleaned before it can be healed otherwise it will keep on festering. Let us cleanse our hearts and our minds and take hands and work together. It is in our hands whether we succeed or not. Let us build a common loyalty towards our country and towards our Province and may God Almighty help us all to heal

> the wounds of the past. In that process we must go forward on the continued road of reform for the better of all the people. Shall we all pray together Nkosi Sikelele i-Afrka. I thank you. (1997)

While Mr. Lategan's speech was much longer than what is quoted, he ultimately came to identify that there was some existing tension coming from the White side of South Africa; that there were a lot of general misunderstandings amongst all South Africans with regards to how the old government worked; and that in order for things to truly be resolved, everyone had to learn to work together without prejudice or resentment. This shifted the discussion away from reparations and toward how the entire community could work together to improve themselves, suggesting a hidden dual purpose to these workshops. They were meant to not only identify and apologize to victims, but to try to rally communities into working together to move past apartheid both socially and with the help of government.

Underlying Problems

One of the more notable reparation cases came from the documentations of Laura Pollecut, a TRC worker who travelled to Pietermaritzburg to interview female victims of various atrocities. It is important to note her foreword at the beginning of the document, where she listed the crimes wrought against these women (some of which included "three [...] widows who had lost their homes, two young girls [...] who had lost their parents plus their homes" [1995:1] and "cases of SADF and SAP harassment and abuse" [1995:1]). Pollecut stated explicitly:

> I am not sure whether all of [these women] can be addressed as the Commission is only really concerned with serious human rights abuses. For example, the whole area of refugees, the majority of which were women, will probably not be perceived as a serious human rights issue. Yet, if one can argue that these women were attacked in their homes, forced to flee, losing all their possessions and their homes, they deserve compensation —reparation. (1995:1).

If this was truly the case of these women, it is questionable as to why their cases have to be argued at all. The document goes on to list several horrible crimes wrought against individual women, in fact. One woman listed grievances such as:

- Her home was attacked and her son was shot. The police took the son and put him in a combi. He was hit and tortured with electric shocks and tubes. A lawyer "stopped" the torture.
- Her house was burnt and in 1990 windows were broken which she then replaced with the help of her brothers. (1995:3.)

While the anonymous woman received small loans and grants to help with the damages, many other woman listed were not nearly as fortunate—if that is even the proper term. There is a clear imbalance here concerning which "gross human rights violations" are actually gross enough to warrant governmental compensation. If we compare this document to the TRC's original proposal, the TRC states:

> Reparation will be given only to those formally declared victims by the Commission. The Commission will decide if someone is a victim by looking at all the information they have on the gross human rights violation suffered by that person. It may be possible, in certain circumstances, that the relatives and dependants of victims will also qualify for reparation. (1995:2.2)

However, if these women's eligibility is dubious, then who qualifies automatically for reparations? Why do some people receive compensation, but not others? Why are some events of human suffering more worthy of aid than others? What is the TRC's criteria for determining who is worthy of reparations? In their original document, the TRC merely stated, "Only people who made statements to the Commission; or were referred to in someone else's statement can be considered for reparation." (1995:2.2) There were no specific requirements, which—especially when looking through the eyes of a victim—is very troubling and lends to doubt and uncertainty for many cases. Upon further investigation, these women were not the only deserving people who may have been excluded from receiving reparations. A 2011 report by the International Center for Transitional Justice outlined the official definition of included victims, as well as the numbers relative to the amount of total victims and which of them received any kind of reparation. The ICTJ—taking reference from the TRC—had this to say about how victims are categorized: "In offering educational and medical benefits to apartheid victims, the regulations define victims as 'those who suffered physical, mental, or emotional injury,' and who either testified before or registered with the TRC prior to the release of its report in 2003." (2011) This definition is still very loose; in addition, acceptance of reparations had long since shut down, which excluded many people who were still in need of explanations, justice, or any kind of aid. The ICTJ went further into their findings, mentioning the Khulumani Support Group—a support group for apartheid victims—in the process:

> The Khulumani Support Group, a 54,000-member organization established in 1995 by survivors and their families, says their records indicate at least 65,000 victims of gross human rights violations covered by the TRC act who should be entitled to reparations. The TRC itself found about 8,000 victims who could have been registered if not for the closing of registration of the victims' list. Thus, if eligibility for reparations is to be based on the closed list, those who received compensation earlier will receive medical and educational benefits while those who were previously omitted will again be excluded from reparations. When we look again at Pollecut's own writings, it begs the question of whether or not these rulings were highly subjective, or if there were other factors involved that kept some victims from receiving reparations. (2011)

In yet another workshop, we do not find citizens discussing reparations in the sense of awards, but through criticizing the TRC's judgment. In a 1997 report titled "Survivors' Perceptions of the TRC and Suggestions for the Final Report," the workers at The Centre for the Study of Violence and Reconciliation and The

Khulumani Support Group recorded their findings upon speaking with members of the Khulumani Support Group. There they found multiple criticisms of how the TRC carried out its decision-making, such as:

- Justice equals Reconciliation: Participants in this group felt that even if perpetrators were held accountable through the amnesty process for their deeds, justice still had to be done. There were strong feelings expressed that perpetrators must be made to contribute materially and financially toward the reparation and rehabilitation of victims. Justice and punishment was still favoured as a way of dealing with the perpetrators over amnesty.
- Reconciliation Is an Individual Process: Some victims/survivors also saw reconciliation as a deeply personal experience and that each and every case must be dealt with individually. Perpetrators must therefore be held accountable individually and be accessible to the victims to meet them.
- Reconciliation Tied-Up with Reparation: A sentiment expressed by most victims/survivors was that reconciliation and reparation were integrally linked. The slogan "No Reconciliation without Reparation" was echoed in many ways throughout the workshops. (1998:2.1.1)

The basic idea here is that the TRC did not do enough. Perpetrators of crimes were not made to physically repent for their wrongdoings, instead being forgiven and let off the hook. Many victims wanted the perpetrators to actually be punished for what they had done, so seeing them simply be let go felt extremely dissatisfying and probably denied them the catharsis they desired or needed to recover. Then, reconciliation between perpetrators and victims were not handled as individual cases, but in group meetings where issues were most likely more cluttered, time was more limited, and victims did not get much chance to have one-on-one discussion with the accused. Lastly, many survivors wanted reconciliation and reparation to be rendered mutually exclusive, rather than an either/or situation where neither option was guaranteed.

The document goes further into the complaints of survivors, creating a summarizing list of what many felt went wrong. Many survivors still felt divided despite the TRC's efforts, and that while the TRC had done well on a national level, they stumbled in resolving things at the community level. Many felt that the TRC was just crossing into new territory in dealing with community-based conflict, and that they could not call themselves done just yet. There were still noticeable gaps between communities, especially between the Coloured and White communities. Citizens noted that there was very little White attendance at workshops. One participant went so far as to comment: "White people do not want to reconcile with blacks since they do not turn up to the TRC meetings." (1998:2.1.2)

Secondly, many survivors thought the way perpetrators were handled was shoddy, because many were left in high-ranking positions, leaving survivors still at their mercy—and while many survivors sought out those who had wronged them, the TRC did little investigation of these offenses. One participant commented on this issue with: "The TRC have not helped with anything here in Duduza. My son was shot. A boy of 15 years—shot with 4 bullets by a policeman. Last year when I went to the police to inquire I was told that the case ended on the 5th of February 1996. The policeman is still working here..." (1998:2.1.2) This issue was similarly touched upon in a political cartoon drawn by Zapiro [that depicted] white perpetrators complaining of the psychological trauma put upon them by the acts they committed during apartheid, and thus being granted reparations along with truly innocent victims. According to the Khulumani report, many victims felt similarly, and thought that perpetrators were secretly being rewarded by the system not only through amnesty, but also through many other ways. One participant said, "Perpetrators are not seen. The government is always begging perpetrators. A lot still needs to be done on the issue of forgiveness" (1998:2.1.2), and yet another commented, "Most perpetrators do not indicate any sign of remorse and are therefore not serious about reconciliation." (1998:2.1.2) This communicates the idea that even reconciliation was not fully achieved; because of perpetrators' failure to even show up to workshops, combined with the TRC's usage of amnesty, shaky deliverance of reparations, and minimal effort in arranging meetings between the victim and their offender, many victims could not see how perpetrators were actually being punished. The Khulumani Group succinctly summarized the participants' opinions as such: "Many participants felt that the TRC has only raised the hopes and aspirations of the people but that tangible results have not emerged; meeting the perpetrator according to the participants was one way this could have occurred." (1998:2.1.2)

Many participants also expressed dissatisfaction with the methods used to inform victims of the workshops and other meetings. The ICTJ criticized more recent methods:

> The DOJ has invited comments on the regulations before June 8, 2011; however, there has been little effort to ensure victims are made aware of the regulations or the deadline to comment. Moreover, given the length and complexity of the regulations themselves and many victims' limited literacy or lack of access to information technology, SATJC is concerned meaningful participation will also be limited. (2011)

Members of the Khulumani Support Group expressed similar views. Many saw the Commission's informational methods as "flawed and inadequate. For example, people indicated that the TRC had hired town councillors (or previous town councillors) to take statements. Victims felt that these individuals did not have a deep interest in the TRC process." (1998:2.1.2)

Because of these factors, analysts such as Nahla Valji felt that the TRC's practices were a grand failure. In her 2003 essay, *South Africa: No Justice without Reparation*, Valji referred to the TRC as a "[deflecting] responsibility from the broader structures of apartheid and those who benefited from them." (2003) This shows from another perspective how deeply the TRC failed to penetrate the existing conflicts within South Africa during the period; Valji outlines a sense of on-going conflict spawned from the aftereffects of the TRC, suggesting a viewpoint that the organization did little to improve the situation.

Conclusion

Annelies Verdoolaege and Paul Kerstens, both African researchers of Belgian descent, describe the TRC's challenges as being determined by factors beyond their control in the 2004 issue of *Africa Today*; specifically, they theorize that the TRC's failures lend to a lack of clear definition of which victims deserved reparations and what these reparations would consist of. (Verdoolaege and Kerstens, 2004:78) Individual reparations were rare because the TRC did not have the finances to award every single victim, so they chose more symbolic methods of reparations. If this is the case, then it is no wonder that many victims still feel as invalidated. While it is true that the government could do so much in such delicate situations, they still do not lend much in the way of aid for victimized civilians.

In the transcript from the 1997 "Forum on Reconstruction and Economic Justice," Professor Heribert Adam expresses his own views on the TRC's handlings:

> We all know that the Truth Commission was a compromise. A compromise between amnesia on the one side, forgetting, and ... back style drives revenge on the other.
>
> I see one fundamental contradiction in how the Truth Commission operates and makes assumption at the moment. The one is, the one fundamental contradiction I see that the more the gory truth comes out the more the victims actually demands justice. And the more the atrocities are revealed the more the perpetrators and the previous system is still legitimised.
>
> So, the truth actually then undermines reconciliation, because neither the victims are satisfied with that compromise nor are the other side who feels that they are de-legitimised. (1997)

This "de-legitimisation" could logically form a dissonance between what the public expects and what the government is truly able to do. Although many problems still exist within South African society, and the government aimed to acknowledge the truth of what happened during apartheid and catalyse the healing process, there was no conceivable way that they could help every single person. The TRC realized this from the start, and this is evidenced clearly enough by the very loose criteria they set at the beginning of the project. While they knew that they only had so many resources to work with, they did not want to shut anyone out from the beginning; however, by their lack of resources they would ultimately have to shut out some people in favour of others. This lends back to the argument that the TRC's endeavour was impossible from the start. The TRC was destined for some amount of failure in terms of granting reparations, because there were just too little resources and too wide a berth of survivors and victims who needed compensation.

Current Controversies

CHAPTER 4

Can Reparations Solve Larger, Systemic Issues?

Overview: Reparations Could Narrow the Racial Wealth Gap

Terry Gross

Terry Gross is a reporter for NPR and hosts the station's popular show Fresh Air.

The killing of George Floyd has ignited protests and inspired conversations—and changes—across the globe. But *New York Times Magazine* writer Nikole Hannah-Jones says more needs to be done to address America's racial wealth gap.

"Very few Americans have created all of their wealth on their own; it's passed down through generations and then built upon," Hannah-Jones says. "Black Americans never really had a chance to do that."

Hannah-Jones traces the wealth gap to slavery, and the fact that enslaved people were not allowed to own property. She notes that the legalized segregation and racial terrorism that followed slavery exacerbated the problem and "prevented generation after generation of Black Americans from acquiring the type of wealth or foothold in the economy that allows you to live a life that is much more typical of white Americans."

Hannah-Jones won a Pulitzer Prize for creating the 1619 Project at the *New York Times*, which tracks the legacy of slavery. Her latest article for the *Times Magazine*, "What Is Owed," makes the case for economic reparations for Black Americans.

"Reparations, to me, is about repair," she says. "In the context specifically of Black Americans, reparations has to do with 250 years of chattel slavery, followed by another 100 years of legalized segregation or apartheid and racial terrorism, and how that impacted the economic well-being of Black Americans."

Interview highlights:

On the Wealth Gap Between White Americans and Black Americans

Black Americans never really had a chance to [create wealth]. Of course, 250 years of slavery where they are unable to accumulate any capital and then coming out of slavery, Black Americans face the dragnet of discrimination and segregation that further prevented them from building any type of wealth. Black people were denied access to colleges, were denied access to high schools, were denied access to higher paying jobs. And when Black people were able to get some land or to build a business, oftentimes they face those businesses being stolen or burned down or destroyed.

So we saw really from 1619 until 1968, when the last of the civil rights legislation was passed saying you could no longer discriminate against Black Americans, Black people being denied access to the primary wealth-building tools, homeownership, federally financed loans, the G.I. Bill to be able to purchase housing that white Americans use to build their wealth. And so what we see today is the stark chasm that was built up over generations, and then only made worse by the fact that today Black Americans still face discrimination across the spectrum of American life.

On Calling for a National Conversation About Reparations

I think that reparations can't just be any one thing. I think that you have to have targeted investment in Black communities and Black schools that have been generationally under-resourced. You certainly need to have a commitment to strong enforcement of existing civil rights laws, because reparations don't do any good if you're still facing rampant employment and housing and educational discrimination. But the center of any reparations program has to be cash payments. The only thing that closes a wealth gap is money.

I think a lot of the times when we have these discussions about, well, let's give scholarships and let's pay for Black people to go to college—one, the facts show that Black people with a college degree still earn less than white people, still have less wealth than white Americans who have a high school degree. So, again, that discomfort with a cash payment is something I think we need to understand is also racialized. And this belief that Black people are not deserving or won't spend their money the way that people think that they should. But you cannot close a racial wealth gap without transferring wealth to the people who have the gap. So cash payments to me have to be central to any program.

On the Conversation About Reparations at the Time of Emancipation

We are often taught in this country that Black people are emancipated and then everyone is on an even footing. We don't often question what does that mean to be emancipated after 250 years of bondage—to be emancipated with no job, no home, no money, no clothes, no bed, no pots, nothing. Enslaved people were unable to own anything or to accrue anything at all. And so what happens at emancipation is this expectation that the government should help formerly enslaved people to get a foothold. And what Black people wanted more than anything was land. ...

So Gen. Sherman takes that to heart and he issues Field Order 15, and Field Order 15 declares that Black families will get 40 acres of former Confederate land, and that they will be able to work that land. ... But unfortunately, that period was very, very brief. President Lincoln was assassinated and he was replaced by his vice president, Andrew Johnson, who was a Southerner who was a white supremacist and who believed, like many white Americans at that time, that Black people were deserving of nothing after slavery, that they should be grateful for their freedom. And he confiscated the land and returned the land to the former confederates. And that ended the only real effort in the history of this country to provide reparations for those who have been enslaved. And that really left formerly enslaved people in absolute devastating poverty. There are stories of mass starvation of Black people after they had been freed, having to leave the plantation and find shelter in burned out buildings, trying to forage for food in burned-out fields. It was a devastating period for Black people. This country decided that it was going to do nothing, that it owed these people nothing.

On Why She Uses the Term "Enslaved Person" and Not "Slave" in Her Writing

It was very important in the 1619 Project and whenever I write about this, to not use language that further dehumanizes people who every system and structure was designed to dehumanize. I think when we hear the word "slave," we think of slavery as being the essence of that person. But if you call someone an enslaved person, then it speaks to a condition. These people were not slaves. Someone chose to force them into the condition of slavery, and that language to me is very important, as is using the word "enslaver" over slave owner because these people didn't have a moral right to own another human being, even though the society allowed it, and I think it needs to be active, that this was an active system of people choosing to treat other human beings as property.

On Where the Concept of the 1619 Project Came From

[As a kid] I never knew that enslaved people, that African people, that my people, had been on this land that long, that we actually arrived here before the pilgrims. And I think I understood even at that moment that there was a reason we had all heard about the ship, the *Mayflower*, and there was a reason none of us had been taught about the ship, the *White Lion*, even though it arrived a year earlier and was just as significant. So that intentional erasure and the power of that erasure stuck with me. ...

So as the 400-year anniversary was approaching, [I] had this nagging feeling in my stomach, a very unsettling feeling that this tremendous anniversary ... that I thought was so foundational to the American story was going to pass, and it was likely going to have very little fanfare. Most Americans probably wouldn't ever even hear of the date. And like so much about the history of Black

Americans and slavery, it was going to be buried and marginalized. And here I am at *The New York Times* and I have a huge megaphone and platform. I could do something about that. But I didn't want it to be a history. ... I wanted to use that anniversary as a time, not to just examine what happened in the past, but to really help us focus on how if you look across modern American life, so much of our institutions, our politics, our culture can be traced back to slavery and bring that story from the margins and make it a central.

On Talking to Her 10-Year-Old Daughter About the Death of George Floyd and the Demonstrations Against Police Brutality

The simple way that you talk about things with a younger child just doesn't work anymore. She wants to know why. And it is the hardest thing as a parent when your child asks you, "Why would that police officer do that to him?" And you don't have an answer because you don't know why. And how do you explain to your child the sweep of 400 years of history that leads this man to think that that would be OK and he wouldn't get in trouble and to feel so little humanity towards this man because he's a Black man?

Those are really hard conversations. And I often wonder if I'm failing at them, if I'm either telling her too much or not explaining it well enough, because, of course, this is tough as a parent ... wanting to protect your child's innocence as long as possible. But being Black in this country and [I understand that] by protecting her too much, I'm actually harming her. I need to prepare her for the world. I need to give her the armor and the language and the understanding to know how the world is going to see her and treat her and people like her. And it's probably one of the things about parenting that I question myself the most [about].

On the Challenge of Having Conversations About Race with White People

I personally don't have a problem talking with anybody about race ... but the challenge—particularly when you're talking to people who are not Black—is the bases of knowledge are just so different. It can be hard to have the same conversation. Black people have to study race. We cannot survive without understanding how race works in this country, without understanding white Americans. It is not a luxury for us not to know, and white Americans can largely exist in society without having to understand that history, without having to understand the social science, really not having to engage [with] it with any level of depth. And so when you're trying to have that conversation, there's so much groundwork that has to come first. And that can be really challenging, because it seems like you can't ever really get to the meat of it.

Then the other thing is, it's very hard for white Americans not to take it personally and get defensive when you're talking about structures that exist and will exist whether an individual person is racist or not. And it speaks to the really superficial way we've dealt with racism in this country, it's either, "Are you saying I'm a bad person?" It's not about that. You don't have to be a bad person to buy a house in a neighborhood that was a creation of racist housing policies. But you are benefiting from those racist housing policies. So I think to me, that is the most challenging part. We don't have a common language and understanding of our history and ... why things are like they are. And a lot of Black folks just get frustrated and don't feel like we should constantly have to teach things that are easy to know.

Reparations Are Necessary, but So Is Even More

Bhaskar Sunkara

Bhaskar Sunkara is a political writer and founding editor and publisher of Jacobin.

The moral case for reparations is undeniable. The United States is a country built in large part off the labor of black slaves. Their coerced labor was turned into capital. That capital was appropriated by planters, filled the coffers of merchants, and fueled industrialists. Meanwhile, the descendants of slaves were stuck of the lowest rung of an incredibly violent and exploitative society.

Even after the tremendous gains of the Civil Rights movement and the election of a generation of black leaders, black Americans have to settle for the worst schools, the worst health care, the worst jobs, and the worst end of the worst justice system in the democratic world. Yet at the same time, they're told by politicians—white and black, Democrat and Republican—that their woes are the product of a "culture of poverty," that they need to just "pull up their pants" and try a little harder.

Far from there being talk of redress for slavery, black Americans have been portrayed as "welfare cheats," dependent on government and unwilling to change their ways.

In this context, the discussion of reparations, sparked by Ta-Nehisi Coates' 2014 essay "The Case for Reparations" and revived in the early days of the 2020 Democratic primary, is welcome. It's good that the distribution of wealth is being discussed as a way to fight racism, rather than merely battles over representation or interpersonal biases.

But reparations can't adequately address racial inequality, can't be effectively administered, and there is still no mass base of black

"To Fight Racism, We Need to Think Beyond Reparations," by Bhaskar Sunkara, Guardian News and Media Limited, March 28, 2019. Reprinted by permission.

Americans pushing for it. We have more effective and popular ways to finally turn America into an egalitarian democracy.

Today, the most prominent mainstream demand for reparations comes from John Conyers's HR 40. It calls for a "commission to study and develop reparation proposals for African Americans to examine slavery and discrimination in the colonies and the United States from 1619 to the present and recommend appropriate remedies." Candidates from across the Democratic field have been asked if they support it, and more generally, reparations. So far the response has been mixed.

Kamala Harris and Elizabeth Warren have embraced the rhetoric of reparations. But both of them seem to just mean they back policies that will disproportionately help black Americans, like tax credits or aid to the victim of housing discrimination. Warren refuses to say she supports direct cash transfers to the descendants of US slaves, but does say it's time for a "full-blown conversation about reparations," including HR 40.

Booker does something similar, he proposes "baby bonds" for every child to address the racial wealth gap, and calls that a "form of reparations." (It isn't.) Sanders says the universal programs he's popularized will help disproportionately marginalized groups but has avoided the reparation rhetoric of other candidates.

His stance is an admirable one, in part because his political brand is based on being straightforward and offering comprehensible solutions to American workers. Supporting a committee just to discuss an issue, or calling policies that aren't reparations "reparations," is the opposite of that approach.

Though he's careful to not say any of the other candidates are a better option for black Americans than Sanders, Coates questions whether Sanders and his staff "understand the illness which they think they can treat through class-exclusive solutions."

I think they do, and that what they're proposing instead represents something radical—a third Reconstruction to finally finish the job of creating democracy in America. The first Reconstruction, which followed the American civil war, was an attempt to use the power of the federal government and the victorious Union army to smash the remnants of planter power and create a new order in the south.

Congressional efforts by radical Republicans took on Lincoln's reactionary successor Andrew Johnson and created the conditions for the newly freed to assert voting rights and win public office. Wealth was redistributed, public schools were erected, and an incredible democratic experiment thrived. A black civil society and politics was created, showing the latent power of those who had been denounced as inferior for generations. This wasn't a cash transfer, it was a revolution.

With this backdrop, figures like the great abolitionist Frederick Douglass foresaw the emergence of "a party in the southern states among the poor," and believed that instead of endless racial animosity, a conflict was brewing "between the wealthy slaveholder and the poor man."

It was a dream stomped out, not by the permanent racist psyche of white Americans, but by a brutal counterrevolution led by powerful southern elites and the terrorism of groups such as the Ku Klux Klan.

But some of the spirit stayed alive, from the multiracial organizing of the Knights of Labor to Populist leaders such as Tom Watson who challenged white and black farmers to "see how this race antagonism perpetuates a monetary system which beggars all."

In time, a second Reconstruction emerged during the civil rights movement of the 1960s that finally won formal equality for black Americans and changed the United States for the better. It fell, however, short of Martin Luther King Jr's hope of not just integrating the lunch counter, but making sure that there was "money to be able to buy a hamburger or a steak." His route to fulfilling this dream was through a labor-based coalition and the fight for an expansive welfare state.

But even if we agree this is important work must be finished, that we must have a new Reconstruction, why not include reparations as part of it? The first case is the technical difficulty of administrating such a program. When it comes to the necessary reparations for the victims of colonialism, we know how to identify those affected and administer redress. The state of France can pay the state of Haiti for its historic crimes, and the state of Haiti can use that wealth (or debt forgiveness) to help spur development that imperialism stunted.

But what kind of bureaucratic process would be necessary to identify who gets to receive the reparations Coates supports? It can't simply be race, because recent immigrants from Africa wouldn't qualify, nor would the descendants of slaves held in former French or British colonies. Would we need a new bureau to establish ancestry? Is that overhead and the work it will involve for black Americans to prove that they qualify worth it compared to creating a universal program that will most help the marginalized anyway?

Or consider this dilemma: money for reparations will come from government expenditure, of which around half is funded by income tax. Could we be in a situation where we're asking, say, a black Jamaican descendent of slaves, or a poor Latino immigrant, to help fund a program that they can't benefit from? Reparations wouldn't be quite such a zero-sum game, but it would hard to shake the perception. Is this really the basis that we can build a majoritarian coalition?

We have a real alternative: solidaristic policies that, unlike reparations, are actually the mass demands of African Americans.

When polled, most black Americans agree that "our society should do whatever is necessary to make sure that everyone has an equal opportunity to succeed" and that government should spend money to tackle poverty. The vanguard of American social democracy, they're joined now by millions of others, commanding majorities that support Medicare for All, a jobs guarantee, free public education, and more.

These are the types of measures that can unite the many against the tiny minority that benefits from their exploitation and continued racialized division.

Are universal programs enough? No, we need to defend affirmative action from right-wing attack and there also needs to be a wider cultural reckoning with slavery. It is outrageous that we live in a former slave state in which there is not a single federal holiday celebrating emancipation. Juneteenth must be enshrined on that basis.

It's also reprehensible that children in American public schools are often given "lost cause" accounts of history that downplay the brutality of slavery or valorize those, like Confederate general Robert E Lee, who murdered to defend it. The education curriculum, by federal mandate, should as rigorously guide the study of slavery in our primary schools as Holocaust studies is guided in Germany. And of course, no statues of Confederate leaders, or those that served the rebel cause, should exist on public land.

But even while we reckon with the history of racism and exploitation, we need to remember that we have a shared destiny. There is still much to do, but through generations of struggle, progress has been made. Racism might seem permanent, but it is an invention of man, not something always to be embedded in our psyches.

HR 40 is a call for a conversation. But what we need more than ever is action. We're closer than we've been in decades to creating the political coalition that can win power and create an egalitarian social democracy in the United States. Such a republic of freedom can't be our final step, but it's the necessary foundation for the world we desperately need, one without race, or class, where life outcomes aren't left to accidents of birth.

How Reparations Can Make Us Whole

Shmuly Yanklowitz

Shmuly Yanklowitz is a notable rabbi and activist.

Hanging in the Museum of Fine Arts in Boston is an indelible, haunting painting. It's a maritime scene: a yellow sun setting above a blood-red sky while hurtling, unruly waves carry an 18th century ship.

These elements don't stir an emotional response, but the foreground does. Among the flotsam are shackles, limbs reaching out from beneath the water, forms of human beings struggling for survival. This is no accident. These remnants are of kidnapped slaves—cruelly thrown off the ship, left to the elements to suffer an ignoble death, brutally rendered in J.M.W. Turner's masterpiece "The Slave Ship."

Like the provenance of the Turner work, American slavery's origins can be accurately traced. An estimated 10 to 12 million kidnapped Africans were transported and shipped via the "Middle Passage" to the New World. About 4 million slaves were sent to the American colonies from the late 15th through the early part of the 19th century.

With a conservative estimate that 1 to 2 million died on the ships, conditions on board are inconceivable to conjure: dignity stripped as humans were chained together, packed tight as if ordinary chattel. Disease was commonplace, the dead and dying (indeed, some of the living) thrown overboard.

Only about 400,000 of the millions of kidnapped Africans ultimately landed in North America (millions went to Brazil), but the legacy of the trans-Atlantic slave trade had a profound impact on the developing American colonies. By the early 1700s, for

"A Rabbi's Plea: We Need Slavery Reparations in Order to Move Forward," by Shmuly Yanklowitz, Yesmagazine.org, June 30, 2015. Reprinted by permission.

example, the population of slaves in South Carolina outnumbered the number of free people.

When we're faced with an image like this one, we are reminded of the barbaric past that influences race relations in the United States today. Could this have been simple greed? Or something more pernicious? Though we are centuries removed from these practices, we are still coming to terms with their legacy. Today, a critical question remains for everyone who enjoys living in a free America: What is my debt to those who involuntarily suffered in the name of liberty and democracy?

This is a difficult question to reconcile. Yet it's clear that the trauma of slavery continues to impact the contemporary American psyche. It is not enough to claim an absolution of blame simply because centuries have passed and society has progressed. Even the election of the first black president, while admirable, is only a single step in the right direction. To be truly accountable, forward-thinking citizens of a liberty-loving nation, we must rectify these inequities. We need reparations.

All too easily, the concept of reparations can be dismissed as a fanciful notion or anti-American. But look at what is happening: America has never addressed past debts in a satisfactory manner, and the strange fruit of our reticence is injurious, de facto discrimination. Eric Garner, Michael Brown, Freddie Gray, and the ensuing strife in Staten Island, Ferguson, and Baltimore are just a few of the examples.

There have long been efforts to bring reparations into focus, but it is a difficult and unpleasant task. This is why the conversation around reparations has to be altered substantially. In Jewish religious and philosophical thought, there is a framework that addresses the concept of not being excused from past debts. Reparations are not punitive; they're restorative.

This idea is mirrored by Professor Mary Frances Berry of the University of Pennsylvania in her call for reparations. "Reparations for unpaid labor are restitution," she says. As the leading advocate for a proposed "reparation superfund," Berry calls for "payment for damages to make whole for harm done." She goes on: "No restrictions should be made on how the money is spent. If their ancestors had received wages for their labor, they too would have bought what they wanted, invested it as they desired, or given it to churches or schools or charities."

Looking below the surface, the economic disequilibrium between whites and blacks is stark. The lack of wealth and economic power in the black community is linked to racial injustices, both obvious and subtle, motivated by unconscious bias. We need a shift in American moral thinking.

There are historical precedents for making reparations. One of the most notable is how Germany acts decades after the events of the Shoah, the Holocaust. Even though German society has evolved considerably and is far removed from those dark events, there is still a desire to show a deep sense of contrition for the evil deeds performed in the name of the nation. Not so long ago, the American government under President Ronald Reagan apologized and gave some compensation to Japanese individuals and their families forced to suffer imprisonment during World War II.

Reparations for slavery are a means to a more just society, not an end to attain absolution. Should we continue to ignore the original turpitude of our founding generations, then we remain complicit. As a Jewish educator, I teach the importance of practicing not only empathy but also action to liberate the enslaved and formerly enslaved. Reparations are our moral responsibility. We must fashion a society that reflects the justice we want to see in the world.

Reparations Are an Idea Whose Time Has Come

Joyce Hope Scott

Joyce Hope Scott teaches African American studies at Boston University.

This is a transformative moment in history in the United States as well as in the rest of the world. Despite myths of a post-racial society as a result of many positive social transformations, we are today again forced to examine our inheritance of America's great sin—slavery and its subsequent legacies of Jim Crow segregation, systemic racism, and dispossession of African Americans. The lens of iPhones, nightly reports by the media, the Black Lives Matter movement, protests against extrajudicial powers of the police, and the murder of Black people with impunity are exposing the fragile underbelly of this society, and what we see is the stark reality of structural racism and visceral inequality.

It is time for truth-telling and acceptance of our moral, legal, political, and sociocultural responsibilities—in essence, another opportunity to acknowledge and make right the deep wrong of chattel slavery and its destructive aftermath for Black people and our entire society. This is an unpopular subject, and Professor Kofi Anyidoho of the University of Ghana noted it best when he remarked that "slavery is like a wound in the belly over which scar tissue has grown. Such a wound is likely to destroy you if it is not opened up and cleaned of its infection." For us in the United States, it lies hidden under the cover of historical amnesia. However, in a 2004 Commencement address at Wellesley College, Nobel Prize winner Toni Morrison reminded us about the deceptive dialectic posed by history, in that: "[T]he past is already in debt to the mismanaged present. And besides, contrary to what you may have heard or learned, the past is not done and it is not over, it's still in process… The past is already changing as it is being reexamined, as it is being listened to for deeper resonances. Actually, it can be more liberating than any imagined future if you are willing to identify its evasions, its distortions, its lies, and are willing to unleash its secrets…"

Dr. Martin Luther King, Jr. (GRS'55, Hon.'59) used the metaphor of unaddressed reparations and restorative justice in his famous 1963 "I Have a Dream Speech," when he declared: "In a sense we've come to our nation's capital to cash a check… America has defaulted on this promissory note insofar as her citizens of color are concerned. Instead of honoring this sacred obligation, America has given the Negro people a bad check which has come back marked 'insufficient funds.'" While Dr. King's metaphor for reparations is articulated in monetary terms, true repair and restorative justice for the damage caused by slavery and its racist legacies can hardly be satisfied by only a check, though that has become the popular image of reparations promoted by its opponents. The financial transaction that assigned the stolen African captives from the slave ship in Baltimore harbor to new "owners" in Charlotte or that resold the chained black child from the slave coffle marching from Washington, D.C., to Mississippi transferred more than a mass of black flesh or legal property. That sale confiscated human beings' rights to life, creativity, production, freedom of movement, and freedom of choice of a mate. It even conveyed to someone else the right to his/her "increase" into perpetuity. Thus, what we must talk about with reparations is what slavery really was—the theft of all rights to life and liberty of those who were enslaved and the subsequent dispossessions of their descendants of psychological, spiritual, and familial connections, and material gain.

This is a litany of civil and human rights violations and a tapestry of looting. In an interview with P. R. Lockhart in *Vox* in August 2019, historian Edward Baptist foregrounds this idea:

"…[P]eople are bought, they're sold, that's the nature of slavery…. But alongside the theft of physical labor, this marks a theft of reproductive labor from enslaved people, and it serves as the crucial engine of the expansion of US slavery." Frederick Douglass made a profound confession of self-theft to his Portsmouth, N.H., audience in 1879 when he acknowledged: "I appear before you this evening as a thief and a robber. I stole this head, these limbs, this body from my master and ran off with them." The trope of theft used here by Douglass captures cryptically the characteristic of that institution from which he escaped and aptly defines the subsequent effects of the legacies of loss from Jim Crow segregation, systemic racism, and inequality on African Americans.

While calls for reparations have a long and varied history (beginning with Belinda Royall/Sutton in 1783), Nora Wittmann, author of *Slavery Reparations Time Is Now: Exposing Lies, Claiming Justice for Global Survival—An International Legal Assessment*, reminds us that the call for reparations for African slavery and restorative justice today is global in its reach and includes "Massive…pollution of our environment, systemic racism, poverty…[police violence and mass incarceration which] have their causes in the current unjust world system…rooted in and…established through transatlantic slavery." She goes on to say: "The formation of legal consciousness about the right to reparations…[is well] anchored in law, and not just demanded by justice and morality."

As part of its agenda during this declared International Decade for People of African Descent, the United Nations commissioned a report which was submitted by its Working Group of Experts on People of African Descent. The group visited several countries, among them the United States, and concluded that the injustice and institutionalized racism they found demonstrates a real problem of Afrophobia and represents a "human rights crisis." They observed that "racial inequality in the US remains a serious challenge as there has been no real commitment to reparations and to truth and reconciliation for people of African descent…

and that contemporary police killings and the trauma it creates are reminiscent of the racial terror lynchings of the past. Impunity for state violence has resulted in the current human rights crisis and must be addressed as a matter of urgency."

Reparations are indeed an idea whose time has come. Advocacy groups like the National African American Reparations Commission (NAARC), National Coalition of Blacks for Reparations in America (N'COBRA), Black Lives Matter Movement, and the Caribbean Community and Common Market (CARICOM) all speak of crimes committed, damages caused, and the structures and compensation needed for Black people to self-repair and advance collectively. The H.R.40 reparations bill of the late US Congressman John Conyers (D-Mich.) acknowledges that the issue of reparations is not just a reference to slavery. The bill, heard by the House Judiciary Subcommittee on June 19, 2019, just months before Conyers' death, seeks to establish a Commission to Study and Develop Reparation Proposals for African-Americans. It declares that the government continued to perpetuate practices disadvantageous to African Americans after the Civil War, including "sharecropping, convict leasing, Jim Crow Segregation, redlining, unequal education, extra judicial lynchings, police violence, and disproportionate treatment at the hands of the criminal justice system." As a result, the bill claims, African Americans "continue to suffer debilitating economic, educational, and health hardships."

When we juxtapose some key images today, one is that of the late iconic Georgia Democratic Congressman John Lewis (Hon.'18) crossing the Edmund Pettus Bridge in Alabama and the other is an image of protestors of all races and ethnicities in the streets of the United States insisting that "Black lives matter" and that there be proper redress of police brutality and justice for the indiscriminate murders of African Americans like George Floyd, Breonna Taylor, Atatiana Jefferson, Aura Rosser, Stephon Clark, Philando Castille, Freddie Gray, Eric Garner, Tamir Rice, Michael Brown, and others. In the final analysis, respect for our moral, social, economic, and political health dictates that there be appropriate efforts of reparatory and transitional justice for the crime against humanity that American chattel slavery and African American dispossession represent. In addition, the marginalization of African American reality in this country invites us all to engage in an in-depth assessment of their experience for the implications it holds for us all—Black and white.

Reparations Are Too Messy to Work

Stuart E. Eizenstat

Stuart E. Eizenstat is a former ambassador to the European Union.

Over the past few years, the idea of reparations for the effects of slavery in the United States has gone from a mostly academic discussion to a political possibility, discussed at presidential debates and in the halls of Congress. This summer, the House held a hearing on a bill, H.R. 40—first introduced in 1989 by Representative John Conyers and reintroduced after his retirement by Representative Sheila Jackson Lee in 2019—that would form a commission to study proposals for how reparations would work in practice. Several of the Democratic Party's candidates for president have said they support the House bill. One of them, Senator Cory Booker, introduced a companion bill in the Senate.

Slavery is a profound historical wrong—one whose brutal legacy permeates American life today. People of color continue to suffer endemic discrimination in employment, housing and new forms of voter suppression. As a result, by every socioeconomic measure—health, education, income, wealth, homeownership and employment levels—they remain far behind white Americans. We must do more to acknowledge, confront and end institutional racial discrimination.

But reparations in the form of cash payments for descendants of slaves are not the way to right this grievous wrong. I write this having spent decades of my life negotiating more than $17 billion in reparations for Holocaust survivors. What I learned as chief negotiator for both the US government, across several presidential administrations, and for the Jewish Claims Conference, a group representing Holocaust survivors in compensation negotiations with the postwar German government, is that reparations are

"What Holocaust Restitution Taught Me About Slavery Reparations," by Stuart E. Eizenstat, *Politico Magazine*, October 27, 2019. Reprinted by permission.

complicated, contentious and messy, and work best when the crime was recent and the direct victims are still alive. Based on my experience, I believe that trying to repay descendants of slaves could end up causing more problems than reparations would seek to solve and that there are better ways to end racial disparities.

To be clear, I am not saying that the horrors of slavery are greater or less than the horrors of the Holocaust. But the fact that slavery is so much farther in the past makes the logistics of reparations next to impossible. Even though some supporters of slavery reparations point to Holocaust reparations as a model, they are actually quite different.

During Bill Clinton's presidency, I served in a newly created position as a special representative of the president and secretary of State on Holocaust-era issues. I led an interagency negotiating team that helped settle a series of class-action lawsuits brought by American lawyers in US courts on behalf of Holocaust survivors or their immediate relatives all over the world against French and Swiss banks. The banks had held funds deposited by Jews seeking to hide them from the Nazis but failed to admit their existence after the war when survivors or direct heirs of victims claimed them; instead, the banks took the money into their own profits. We also settled class-action lawsuits against European insurance companies that refused to pay beneficiaries on the specious ground that premiums were not paid while policyholders were in concentration camps. We obtained payments from hundreds of German and Austrian companies that employed Jewish slave laborers, working them to death, and non-Jewish forced laborers from Poland and other countries overrun by the Nazis. All worked under brutal conditions but were viewed as wartime assets to substitute for German men conscripted to fight. We also arranged for the restitution of private property in Austria, compensation or recovery of thousands of Nazi-looted artworks, and the return of synagogues, community centers and even cemeteries confiscated by the Nazis and nationalized by postwar communist governments.

During the Obama administration, in 2014, when I continued this work as special adviser to Secretaries of State Hillary Clinton and John Kerry, we negotiated reparations for non-French citizens from the French government for deporting Jewish residents to death camps aboard the state-owned railway and for their spouses and children if they survived the war but died before our agreement. Since 2009, I have also led annual negotiations with Germany on behalf of the Conference on Jewish Material Claims Against Germany and obtained payments for pensions, home care, food and medical services for survivors in or near poverty. Overall, we have managed to obtain a degree of justice—even if it is imperfect. It took decades and is still a painstaking process.

The common thread running through these US-led negotiations and those of the Claims Conference is that restitution has come from the direct perpetrators of the crimes and has gone largely to those who directly suffered and survived, and, in some cases, their direct heirs. And even this was extremely difficult. In the Austrian property cases, there were 18,000 claims filed—largely by heirs of victims—with the Austrian claims process having to sort out competing claims among families. Controversy arose in the French railway case because payments went only to living survivors of the deportations or their spouses or children if the deportee had died after World War II and before our agreement; distant relatives of deportees were excluded.

Imagine how these problems would be compounded in any program of individual reparations for descendants of slaves. Under such a program, a direct link would be necessary to prove which of today's 37 million African Americans would be eligible for reparations. But poor record-keeping during the slavery era, which predated America's founding, makes it extremely difficult to trace ancestry back to a specific slave family. With Holocaust-era slave laborers, we applied a sort of "rough justice" by using Red Cross and German concentration camp records to pay a flat sum of $7,500 to each former inmate, regardless of how long they had been held captive (forced laborers received $2,500). It is hard to see how such an approach would work in America, where slave records are flawed and far from complete. That system would also disadvantage those African Americans unable to establish such a linkage because they lacked the economic wherewithal to pursue the difficult genealogical task or because records did not exist.

Other US government reparations programs have stuck to paying direct victims or their immediate family. More than 100,000 Americans of Japanese descent who were interned during World War II were each paid $20,000 under a law signed in 1988 by President Ronald Reagan, but nothing was paid to the heirs of those who died before the 1988 law went into effect. The benefits from the settlement of the lawsuit dealing with the awful government experiment at Tuskegee University that withheld treatment for syphilis from hundreds of black patients went only to survivors, their wives and widows, or their children.

Then there is the question of costs. Germany has paid more than $60 billion since 1952 for the horrors of the Holocaust and continues to this day to provide for those living survivors in special need, but not their descendants. Economic estimates of the potential cost of reparations for distant heirs of slaves range from about $500 billion to as high as $17 trillion, which is more than three times current annual federal spending. Who would pay for this? All American taxpayers would have to bear the burden of reparations, perversely including many of the intended beneficiaries.

There are a few problems with this. For one, such an expensive, taxpayer-funded program stands little to no chance of being enacted. A Gallup Poll shows a majority of Americans, 67 percent, say the government should not arrange cash payments for slavery. But also, rather than promote the reconciliation we so badly need, reparations could seriously inflame racial tensions, stoking the resentment of nonblack citizens who would feel their needs for government assistance were being ignored in a rapidly changing, dislocating economy. According to that same Gallup Poll, only 16 percent of white Americans support cash reparations, while 73 percent of African Americans do. A government program white citizens perceive to be helping African Americans at their expense, for a crime they did not commit, would only push them further from understanding racism in America.

Some have suggested that the best reparations policy would dole out payments to all African Americans in the United States, regardless of whether they could prove their descent from slaves. But the costs for this would be even greater, making it even more politically improbable. Not to mention that any such plan risks further worsening race relations.

Part of what makes slavery reparations impractical is also what makes slavery's legacy so insidious and difficult to combat. We're not talking about a single, horrific, recent event. Slavery began before the founding of the country and continued for centuries. It ended more than a century ago. But its trauma has persisted for generations, continuing to harm African Americans even as it has become less visible to other Americans.

With this in mind, there are better ways to promote the healing this country needs than a formal reparations program. More feasible and urgent would be committing the nation to reducing inequality in income and wealth by making targeted and thoughtful investments to lift up both low-income communities and communities of color—an approach already favored by many of the Democratic candidates. That should include strengthening our national safety net. The government should also set aside additional federal funding for historically black colleges and black entrepreneurs as well as commit to stricter enforcement of discriminatory lending practices and to strengthening the 1965 Voting Rights Act to empower the federal government to protect African Americans against a withering variety of voter suppression efforts.

Two presidents from the South, Lyndon B. Johnson and Jimmy Carter, supported a range of policies to help increase opportunities for African Americans. Carter enforced set-asides for minority contractors on federal projects and affirmative action in admission to colleges. Both presidents supported funds for race-neutral, income-based programs, too: Public-private partnerships for investment in low-income areas, Head Start classes for disadvantaged children, Title I of the Elementary and Secondary Education Act for schools with high percentages of low-income students, and Pell Grants for college aid to needy students. President Barack Obama's Affordable Care Act, with its broadened coverage for private health insurance and expanded Medicaid benefits, is another more recent example of a program that helps minorities but also targets Americans in need regardless of race. The Trump administration has opposed most of the special affirmative action programs and has sought to cut the budgets for many of these programs. Instead, these programs should be continued and enhanced.

Education about the injustice of slavery and continued discrimination is also crucial. Just as the US Holocaust Memorial Museum in Washington has drawn more than 50 million visitors—three-quarters of them non-Jews—and teaches the causes and effects of the Holocaust, the magnificent new National Museum of African American History and Culture that stands on our National Mall educates overflow crowds about slavery and its impact and also the great contributions of African Americans to every field of American endeavor. The International Holocaust Remembrance Alliance, an organization I helped create with the leadership of then-Swedish Prime Minister Göran Persson, now has 33 countries promoting Holocaust education. In America, the Department of Education and state educators should develop model courses on the realities and legacies of slavery and discrimination.

A large part of the argument for reparations is the symbolic importance of an admission of wrongdoing. Public apologies can be powerful tools for reconciliation, too. The Japanese American reparations legislation signed by Reagan included a national apology, and Bill Clinton formally apologized on behalf of the US government for the unethical experiments on black men with syphilis at the Tuskegee Institute. Nine states, including former Confederate states of Alabama, North Carolina and Virginia, have formally apologized for slavery. The US House and Senate passed bipartisan resolutions of apology in 2008 and 2009 but failed to reconcile the two versions and send them to the president. No US president has ever formally apologized for slavery. It is time for another effort.

The best model for helping overcome prejudice and hate is South Africa's Truth and Reconciliation Commission. Its mandate from Nelson Mandela included neither financial compensation for apartheid nor punitive measures against its white perpetrators. The commission took testimony from 20,000 victims and from those who did evil deeds, under a provision of amnesty. In accepting the commission's report, Mandela majestically declared its purpose was "to help reconcile and build our nation," to heal and not to divide. It gave black citizens of South Africa the feeling that they could air their grievances in a constructive way, to demonstrate the evils of apartheid on an individual and collective basis. At the same time, it avoided direct retribution against its white perpetrators, curbing resentment and risk of making racism even worse and set a course for a degree of racial reconciliation during Mandela's tenure as president.

We need a similar commission in the United States to examine slavery and racial discrimination to expose hidden truths, past and present, not for divisive individual or group compensation.

I'm not saying this will all be easy or that it won't be politically divisive. Policies like expanding the social safety net and cracking down on voter suppression face significant political headwinds, a congressional and presidential apology for slavery and a reconciliation commission would face headwinds in today's polarized political environment. But I believe that politicians are much more likely to push for—and Americans are much more likely to accept—these efforts than cash payments for descendants of slaves.

The concept of reparations for what Abraham Lincoln called "the bondsman's unrequited toil" is at least as old as the immediate post-Civil War years, when in 1865, General William Tecumseh

Sherman issued a field order offering the freed slaves 40 acres of land and army mules as a step toward self-sufficiency, economic inclusion and redress. But Lincoln's successor, President Andrew Johnson, annulled Sherman's order after Lincoln's assassination, and in 1872, the Freedmen's Bureau, created by Congress to help freed slaves enter the economic mainstream, was closed.

It's time for the country to get serious about making up for that mistake—and for the decades of mistakes and discrimination that followed. But we should pick a way forward that avoids sending the country into a divisive, complicated, contentious process that could bog down our politics for decades.

Can Reparations Correct Something Like the Tulsa Massacre?

Mihir Desai and Brian Kenny

Mihir Desai is a professor at Harvard Business School. Brian Kenny is the chief marketing and communications officer there.

Survivors of the 1921 Tulsa Massacre and their descendants believe historic social injustices should be addressed through reparations. Professor Mihir Desai discusses the arguments for and against reparations in response to the Tulsa Massacre and, more broadly, to the effects of slavery and racist government policies in the US in his case, "The Tulsa Massacre and the Call for Reparations."

[...]

Brian Kenny: [...] We've heard throughout this month, the past month, we've been featuring cases with Black protagonists, and we did one on incarceration in the United States, and the Jim Crow laws have been a consistent theme throughout those. So the damage obviously in this country for African-Americans has continued well beyond 1865 and up to this day. And that's part of the reason why it's important to write cases like this and to talk about cases like this in educational institutions around the country. Let's take a look at Oklahoma in the late 1800s, because I thought Oklahoma was an unlikely place to have a gathering of African-Americans when most of them were brought into the US and moved to the Southern part of the country to work on plantations. How did they end up in Oklahoma?

Mihir Desai: Yes. So it turns out Oklahoma's completely fascinating. So it's a part of the United States that doesn't become a state until

1907. And prior to that, in fact, throughout the 1800s, was known as the Indian Territories. And it evolved from the forced resettlement, or the Trail of Tears of five tribes, five Native American tribes, who were forcibly resettled into what came to be known as Oklahoma. So beginning in the late 1800s, 1889 or 1890, it was opened up for settlement. And so whites and Blacks started to move into Oklahoma. And in fact, some Blacks had been enslaved in the Indian Territories.

And then many Blacks sought to go to Oklahoma, in some sense, to actually free themselves from the Jim Crow of the south. Of course, whites did as well and there was a huge amount of racial tension that popped up as both these communities migrated into the Indian Territory. And then of course the last piece of the puzzle is Oklahoma then had just an enormous boom because of oil. And so a number of Native American tribes benefited from this, or at least became richer because of it. And then Blacks and whites also migrated there very quickly, especially to Tulsa, to try to capitalize on the oil boom. And Blacks in particular saw it as an opportunity to create communities that were holistic and that recycled their profits and their capital within that community to create vibrancy. And that's precisely what happened in Greenwood and with Black Wall Street.

Brian Kenny: So talk a little bit about Greenwood, how did it come to be known as the Black Wall Street, and what were the conditions that made it possible for entrepreneurship to thrive with that community?

Mihir Desai: Yes, so it's a great story. So the name Black Wall Street actually came about because Booker T. Washington went there and just saw the wealth that was there. There was no particular financial element to it, but just that Blacks had been so successful in creating economic vibrancy there. There were a couple of particular Black entrepreneurs who bought a bunch of land, and then basically leased it out to other Blacks, creating effectively a Black community in Greenwood. And there was just a remarkable set of data about how well-educated they were, relative to the rest of Oklahoma and the rest of the country, how high quality the housing was, how much entrepreneurship there was. Real businesses, theaters, professionals, doctors, all kinds of things.

And in fact, that's one of the striking things in the multimedia case, because Ruth created this wonderful montage of what Black Wall Street looked like, and it is just a reminder of how vibrant that community was and how much entrepreneurship there was.

Brian Kenny: So here's this thriving community that we didn't know about until very recently. And we don't want to paint the picture that things were great in Oklahoma for Blacks, because as you say, they weren't. I was surprised to see in the exhibits the number of lynchings. Outside of the southern states, Oklahoma I think had the highest number of lynchings of any northern state. Is that accurate?

Mihir Desai: Lynchings were common throughout the South, but within the rest of the country, they were there, and in Oklahoma in particular. And that really, I think, set the stage for what ended up being these riots and the massacre, which is lynchings are a very disturbing part of our past, but it's really important to come to terms with, which is kind of an extra judicial system of capital punishment that was being run against Blacks. And the fear of it, because it was so commonplace, was so understandable. Because it happened all the time. And then of course that fear combined, of course, with the underlying tension is what really sparks the Tulsa Massacre itself.

Brian Kenny: Let's talk about then, after the riot happens, Greenwood is essentially burned to the ground. There's really not much of anything left there. People have lost their homes and their fortunes and they are now homeless. What is the economic fallout of something like that?

Mihir Desai: Well, in some sense it's incalculable because of the loss of life and because of the dashing of just remarkable amounts of motivation and dreams. But there were very specific claims, property damages. And it's really quite remarkable because despite the fear that they must've felt, the survivors filed the claims. Filed the claims against the city, filed claims against the state for the destruction of wealth. And in today's dollars, the claims that they filed are on the order of 30 to 40 million dollars of real specific property damage. Unfortunately, those cases never really went anywhere. And in fact, there was no meaningful effort to really think through addressing those crimes until the 1990s.

So the damage is enormous from a financial and economic perspective, but the psychological damage, the loss of life, is really, I think, incalculable. But the interesting thing from the perspective of reparations, and the reason I really wanted to use the case both to explore Tulsa, but also reparations is here is a situation where there's a very specific property claim, and there's a very specific set of actions by governmental actors. And some of them, at least up until recently, some of them were alive. The survivors were alive. So by looking at reparations in this case, one can then pivot to the broader question of reparations, which is much, much harder. But the reparations part of the case really starts with the specificity of Tulsa, but then moves to this bigger issue where reparations gets even thornier, because time has passed. Because the people who might have done these things are gone. Because the people who these things were done to may be gone, and then reparations becomes even thornier than it is in the Tulsa case.

Brian Kenny: Yes. And we've heard reparations shows up in the news quite frequently around the world, and the case dives into some examples of where reparations have been discussed and in some places have been implemented. Can you just talk, I guess pull the lens back a little bit and talk about what the essence of reparations, what are they, what are they intended to do, and where have they been applied and been successful?

Mihir Desai: Yes, it's a fascinating history, and I'm really proud of this part of the case, which is to look for parallels and to think about this in a global perspective. And in fact, you mentioned I taught this last week. It was so interesting to get the reactions of international students, who brought up so many examples of this, which I didn't cover in the case. But so for example, there's the example of "los desaparecidos" or the disappeared people in Chile. There's the example of caste in India. There's the example of the so-called comfort women in Japan.

So this is an issue that's really widespread, which is what do you do with these historic injustices? We have these examples. There's one relatively small example in the United States which parallels Greenwood, which is a community in Florida known as Rosewood, where they in fact did succeed in getting reparations for a somewhat similar event. There's of course, the remarkable set of events associated with the Japanese Americans and their internment, which is again, historically not been taught very much. But we found our way to providing cash payments to the survivors of those Japanese American internment camps. This was of course at the time of World War II, but by the 1980s we figured out how to do that. We have the example of German reparations for Holocaust survivors. And then of course we have the Truth and Reconciliation Commission in South Africa.

It's hard to talk about them as successful, Brian, in the sense that there's so much difficulty around these issues and it is not as if reparations undo what happened. But they can potentially serve to first remind us all of what happened, address the remarkable amount of damage that was done, and provide a real acknowledgement of it. But in America, we've really struggled with this question.

It's very hard to combine that heroic narrative with a recognition of the horrible things that have been done alongside it. And that I think is what is really tough about this. And by the way, there are very good arguments for reparations and very good arguments against them. This is not a clear-cut question by any stretch, and what the case really tries to do more than anything else is allow us to begin creating the language to address whether it's a good idea or not.

Brian Kenny: Well, fraught politically. Every example you've given there are political implications to those. There are certainly people who will say, "I wasn't alive when that happened. I wasn't responsible. Can't blame me for what happened 100 years ago." So I'm curious. You said there are very good reasons to oppose reparations. What are some of the good reasons? Because the ones I just cited aren't very good.

Mihir Desai: So the first one is that as time passes, the validity of these claims goes away, and we have to, instead of being preoccupied with injustices from 200 years ago, we have to address today's and think about them today, and we have to be forward-looking.

There's a concern that this will serve to absolve communities of their ongoing responsibilities to racial subgroups that continue to be disenfranchised in one or another way. So there's an interesting discussion about the debt and the deficit in this kind of setting, which is by focusing so much on these historic injustices, will we obscure actually ongoing things that are happening that really merit our attention? In fact, the mayor of Tulsa has said that cash payments to the descendants of survivors will only divide us.

One advocate against reparations, Coleman Hughes, has I think very evocatively put it and said that justice for the dead will come at the expense of justice for the living. And if you're for reparations, I think you have to take on those arguments. Part of the idea of the case is to make you aware of them and take them on. But of course the arguments for reparations are also very important and compelling, which is, we can't move on until we repair this part of our past. And no acknowledgement is full enough without a cash payment. And in fact, damages were done to these people. Economic damage was done to these people.

And of course the legacy is ongoing and is not limited to Tulsa. It is not limited to slavery. It goes all the way through the

20th century with housing policies and financial access issues, and wealth has been mal-distributed because of those ongoing injustices. And so if you're against reparations, I think you have to address all those arguments as well, because those are really powerful, real arguments also.

Brian Kenny: You mentioned Rosewood, Florida, which is another historical situation that I didn't know about until I read the case, and reparations were also asked for in that case, but there was a subtle difference to the reparations that were being looked for in Oklahoma. Can you maybe break that down a little bit?

Mihir Desai: Sure. So the Rosewood example is a really interesting counterexample to Greenwood. So Rosewood is in Florida, and similar circumstances on the underlying tragedy, but in the late 1990s, the Florida legislature provided reparations for the descendants of, and the survivors of Rosewood. And I think there's two issues there. One is there's just sheer political power, which is the ability of Blacks to mobilize and to effectuate political change in legislature, given the demographics of Florida, is just far greater than in Oklahoma.

And then the second part of it is, and this is what's really interesting for the reparations debate more generally, which is they really framed it up in terms of a property issue, and not in terms of a racial justice issue. And I think there are people who look at the two contrasting outcomes and say, "Well, when you frame it up as property, you're more likely to win. And when you frame it up as racial justice, maybe you're not."

And of course goes to the broader reparations debate, which is, are we trying to correct a historic injustice associated with, for example, wages not being paid for slavery, or for example, wealth not created because of FHA rules? Or are we trying to equalize Black and white household wealth, and trying to address racial justice today? Those are two very, very different arguments.

Brian Kenny: Right. So property framing is less racially charged, but therefore it is a less powerful argument in terms of racial justice. That's what I'm hearing.

Mihir Desai: Yes. And that's the kind of conundrum here, which is this: The path that may be more successful isn't as rewarding in some ways, as well.

[…]

As a Legal Process, Reparations Will Never Happen

Darren Zook

Darren Zook teaches politics and human rights at the University of California, Berkeley.

[…]

The stark reality, however, is this: reparations will never happen in America. Indeed, they *can't* happen, for reasons I will explain in excruciating detail. What is perhaps most surprising and disheartening is that any effort to pay reparations will crumble in the courts because the paying of reparations itself will be ruled an injustice. That may seem entirely counterintuitive, if not outright contradictory, so let me reiterate once again my observation about law and justice: what we want the law to say and what it actually says are rarely the same thing.

The reason that the payment of reparations will be ruled an injustice is because the act will not hold up to the principles of justice in terms of both process and substance. If you're wondering how on earth it would be possible that an act designed to remedy the injustice of slavery could itself be ruled itself an injustice, we have to first understand how the law works and how the law thinks. Understanding these two things is the key to understanding everything about reparations and why they will never happen.

[…]

Reparations Are a Legal Process

Reparations are part of a larger area of legal action that is referred to as remedy. Acts of remedy can also include: (1) restitution, which is the relinquishing and transfer of unjust gains to the rightful

"Why Reparations Will Never Happen," by dczook, Medium, July 25, 2019. Reprinted by permission.

claimant; (2) compensation, which is the transfer of property, usually in the form of financial transfer, to a claimant who has been unjustly deprived of some form of tangible property; or (3) satisfaction, which can include a formal apology for a wrongful and unjust act. Reparations as an act of remedy refer to the provision of recompense for an unjust act where the original tangible property cannot be recovered or where the cost cannot be precisely valued (for example, reparations for war).

So what's the problem, one might ask? Slavery was clearly an unjust practice, depriving thousands of persons of life, liberty, and property, so some form of remedy is clearly in order, and reparations seem to fit the situation perfectly. This, however, is where we have to look closely at how the law actually works and what the law actually says. *Unjust* in the context of remedy means only and precisely *legally* unjust, meaning the act in question was considered unjust in accordance with law. In simpler terms, it means the act in question must have been illegal when it was committed.

What that means in practice is that the first question any institution of law must necessarily ask in considering the issue of reparations is whether or not the act in question was an illegal act. More specifically in relation to the issue of reparations, that question looks like this: was slavery illegal in the United States or in any other legal pact of which the United States was a legal signatory when the slave trade occurred and when slavery was implemented in the United States? The answer to this question is legally unequivocal: no, it was not illegal. That fact alone is probably sufficient for any court of law in the United States to nullify a claim for reparations for slavery.

[…]

What About Human Rights?

If American law fails us on this, it would be understandable for anyone, spurred on perhaps by an unbearable sense of frustration, to turn to the more universal principles of human rights to search for some possibility for remedy. And indeed, a quick look at the

Universal Declaration of Human Rights (UDHR, 1948) will reveal that Article 4 states in very specific terms that "no one shall be held in slavery or servitude; slavery and the slave trade shall be prohibited in all their forms." So there it is—slavery is clearly a human rights violation, so reparations are back on the table as a human rights issue, right?

Unfortunately, here, too, the law does not give us what we want. For one thing, the UDHR is actually not a legally-binding document (declarations are not treaties). The good news is that we do have a human rights treaty that translates the moral principles of the UDHR into legal ones, and that treaty is the International Covenant on Civil and Political Rights (ICCPR, entered into force in 1976), of which Article 8 legally prohibits slavery and the slave-trade in all its forms. The bad or sad news, however, is that this is still of no help in our quest to find a legal foot in the door for the claim of reparations for slavery in America.

There are two specific reasons for this. The first comes in the form of a fundamental principle of law that is considered for the most part inviolable: in its original Latin form, and it is almost always invoked in Latin, it reads *nullem crimen sine lege*, or "no crime without (the) law." What this means in more colloquial terms is that law cannot be applied retroactively, as in, the act in question had to be illegal by the laws in place at the time it was committed to be considered a crime. As a simple example, it works like this: if the speed limit is lowered from 70 mph to 60 mph today and the police caught you on camera doing 70 mph yesterday, the police cannot charge you with speeding as the law was not yet in force. Remedy does not apply to acts that were legal at their time of commission.

[…]

Can't We Just Bypass the Courts?

To get right to the point, no, we can't. A person might understandably think that if law is so obsessed with the meticulous details of procedure and evidence that it can't render justice for what is clearly an historical injustice, why don't we just elect a

Democratic president who can invoke reparations as an act of executive privilege, or elect a Democratically-controlled House and Senate that can pass through a bill for a reparations? Even if both of those happen after the November 2020 elections, reparations still won't happen because the act of executive privilege or the passing of a congressional bill will immediately be challenged and the challenge will go directly to the courts. The evidence for this is quite obvious: think of how many times the courts have stepped in to rule on challenges against any one of Trump's policies, even those enacted by executive privilege.

[...]

Politics

We also have to remember that the reason that reparations are now very much in public parlance is because several Democratic presidential candidates have said they would push for reparations if elected. This is largely because the Democratic party has pretty much only one goal at this point, which is to push for the opposite of anything Trump wants or is.

Politics in America, however, is a wily creature, and the issue of reparations could become a minefield for the Democrats and a gold mine for the Republicans. The Republicans can (and probably will) point out that it was the Democratic Party that supported slavery, and the Republicans who supported abolition. Anyone who knows the history of the 13th Amendment, the Amendment that ended slavery, knows that initially it was defeated in the House—Republicans voted for it (meaning they wanted to abolish slavery), while Democrats largely voted against it. "Look at the hypocrisy of those Democrats," the Republicans will say on the trail to November 2020— "pro-slavery when that gets the vote, and pro-reparations when that gets the vote. Sad!" It doesn't matter that such a claim requires a tremendously skewed re-reading of American political history. There are unfortunately more than enough voters who haven't read much of American history to allow the claim to stick and wreak its deceptive damage.

Also, keep in mind that no Democratic candidate has actually promised to pay reparations if elected, and this is a crucial point everyone needs to understand, because it will certainly come out the closer we get to November 2020. What those Democratic presidential candidates who support reparations have actually said is that if they are elected they will "appoint a commission" to "consider the issue." If you are wondering why no candidate has said in unequivocal language that they will promise to pay reparations if elected, it's because they either have a law background (Kamala Harris) or have legal advisors on their campaigns who know that reparations will never pass legal scrutiny. To "appoint a commission," however, is a promise that a candidate can follow through on—it secures the votes first, and then delivers the commission's foregone conclusion (most likely in some neutral language such as "the commission's results were inconclusive") after the election is over and power has already been secured. In simpler terms, the issue of reparations is a political strategy designed to buy votes.

[...]

Organizations to Contact

The editors have compiled the following list of organizations concerned with the issues debated in this book. The descriptions are derived from materials provided by the organizations. All have publications or information available for interested readers. This list was compiled on the date of publication of the present volume; the information provided here may change. Be aware that many organizations take several weeks or longer to respond to inquiries, so allow as much time as possible.

American Descendants of Slavery

Chicago, IL 60619
email: info@adoschicago.org
website: www.adoschicago.org
One of the primary groups aimed at organizing Americans who are descendants of enslaved people, this group has long had reparations as a key tenet of its platform. The group, however, has attracted some controversy for its insistence that Black Americans are fundamentally distinct from both Africans and people who later immigrated voluntarily.

The Charles Hamilton Houston Institute for Race and Justice

Harvard Law School
Areeda Hall, Room 522
1545 Massachusetts Avenue
Cambridge, MA 02138
(617) 495-8285
email: houstoninst@law.harvard.edu
website: www.charleshamiltonhouston.org
The latest project of Harvard Law professor Charles Ogletree, this organization follows in the footsteps of the group Ogletree founded at the turn of the 2000s: the Reparations

Coordinating Committee. That group had been formed to explore if reparations were possible through legal means.

Equal Justice Initiative Lynching Memorial and Museum

115 Coosa Street
Montgomery, AL 36104
(334) 386-9100
email: ticketing@eji.org
website: www.museumandmemorial.eji.org
The first memorial in the country dedicated to acknowledging the victims of racial terror lynchings throughout American history, the Montgomery, Alabama-based project opened in 2018. The project was convened with the idea of creating "a sober, meaningful site where people can gather and reflect on America's history of racial inequality."

International Network of Scholars and Activists for Afrikan Reparations

50 George Square
Newington, Edinburgh EH8 9JU
United Kingdom
+44 131 651 5984
email: dashkova.centre@ed.ac.uk
website: www.inosaar.llc.ed.ac.uk
This group formed in 2017 at the University of Edinburgh in order to assist in the consolidation of the "growing Afrikan global reparations movement." The group says that it sees reparations as "a useful tool for considering repair and restorative justice for the crimes against humanity that chattel slavery represents."

National Black United Front

17 Academy Street
Newark, NJ 07102
(800) 223-0866
email: information@babuf.org (Bay Area branch)
website: www.nbuf.org

Formed in the late '70s, this group is one of the earliest contemporary groups to focus on the idea of reparations and, today, still has multiple branches spread around the United States. These days, the group's primary aims include "self-help, economic opportunity, positive community change and social justice."

National Coalition of Blacks for Reparations in America

PO Box 90604
Washington, DC 20090
(202) 643-1460
email: info@ncobraonline.org
website: ncobraonline.org

Founded in 1987, this group identifies as the "premiere" coalition of organizations organized for the sole purpose of obtaining reparations for African descendants in the United States. The group has chapters, members, affiliates, and supporters throughout the country, as well as ones in Africa, Europe, Central and South America, and the Caribbean.

The National Coalition of Churches for Reparations

1000 S. 4th Street
Louisville, KY 40203
(502) 776-1443, ext. 5130
email: contact@nccfr.org
website: nccfr.org

This nonprofit tasked itself with mobilizing Christian churches in support of reparations for descendants of slavery in the US. The group was founded by a group of religious students who say they had dedicated their studies to the work of Yvette Carnell, the cofounder of a different reparations group called the American Descendants of Slavery.

National Legal and Policy Center

107 Park Washington Court
Falls Church, VA 22046
(703) 237-1970
email: nlpc@nlpc.org
website: nlpc.org

A right-wing think tank that promotes criticism of liberal ideas, this group has been among the staunchest opponents of reparations in the current political landscape, namely publishing a 2004 monograph called "The Case Against Slave Reparations," widely cited by those making that case. In the time since, the group and its organization have circulated similar arguments with titles like "Reparations: Blueprint for a Shakedown" and "Socialism: A Youthful Passion, A National Problem."

RepAfrika

15 Bartholomew Row
Birmingham B5 5JU
United Kingdom
email: aissata.repafrika@gmail.com
website: www.inosaar.llc.ed.ac.uk/en/repafrika

The self-described "youth wing" of the International Network of Scholars and Activists for Afrikan Reparations, RepAfrika formed in 2018 at Birmingham City University and, per its guidelines, forbids membership to anyone over the age of 40. Among its numerous goals, the group aims to find funding that would be to "uplift Afrikan Reparatory Justice Projects" and that would result in an "Afrikan-friendly environment in both traditional and non-traditional academic spaces."

The Task Force to Study and Develop Reparation Proposals for African Americans

PO Box 820200
Sacramento, CA 94203
(916) 322-3360
email: ReparationsTaskForce@doj.ca.gov
website: https://oag.ca.gov/ab3121
In 2021, California Governor Gavin Newsom established a nine-person task group to study how reparations could be implemented by the state. The group includes descendants of enslaved people who are now prominent lawyers, academics, and politicians, and the group is aimed at establishing a framework for how governments can realistically approach the issue.

The UN's International Decade for People of African Descent

405 East 42nd Street
New York, NY, 10017
(212) 963-7160
email: inquiries2@un.org
website: www.un.org/en/observances/decade-people-african-descent
In 2014, the United Nations announced that the following decade would be the "International Decade for People of African Descent." For the international human rights organization, this means meetings on the subject of "elaborating a United Nations declaration, which is the first step towards a legally binding instrument, on the promotion and full respect of human rights of people of African descent," and this involves the release of a vast trove of resources on the history of the slave trade and how those injustices are seen in a current light.

Bibliography

Books

Ana Lucia Araujo. *Reparations for Slavery and the Slave Trade: A Transnational and Comparative History*. London, UK: Bloomsbury Publishing, 2017.

Fernne Brennan. *Race Rights Reparations: Institutional Racism and the Law*. Milton Park, UK: Taylor & Francis, 2017.

Roy L. Brooks. *Atonement and Forgiveness: A New Model for Black Reparations*. Berkeley, CA: University of California Press, 2019.

J. Angelo Corlett. *Race, Racism, and Reparations*. Ithaca, NY: Cornell University Press, 2018.

Katherine Franke. *Repair: Redeeming the Promise of Abolition*. Chicago, IL: Haymarket Books. 2019.

Sarah Goldy-Brown. *Reparations for Slavery: The Fight for Compensation*. New York, NY: Lucent Press, 2017.

Rhoda E. Howard-Hassmann and Anthony P. Lombardo. *Reparations to Africa*. Philadelphia, PA: University of Pennsylvania Press, 2018.

Duke L. Kwon and Gregory Thompson. *Reparations: A Christian Call for Repentance and Repair*. Grand Rapids, MI: Baker Publishing Group, 2021.

Jesse McCarthy. *Who Will Pay Reparations on My Soul? Essays*. New York, NY: W. W. Norton & Company, 2021.

A. Kirsten Mullen and William A. Darity Jr. *From Here to Equality: Reparations for Black Americans in the 21st Century*. Chapel Hill, NC: University of North Carolina Press, 2020.

Alondra Nelson. *The Social Life of DNA: Race, Reparations, and Reconciliation After the Genome*. Boston, MA: Beacon Press, 2016.

Andre M. Perry. *Know Your Price: Valuing Black Lives and Property in America's Black Cities*. Washington, DC: Brookings Institution Press, 2020.

Raymond Winbush. *Should America Pay? Slavery and the Raging Debate on Reparations*. New York, NY: HarperCollins, 2010.

Stephanie Wolfe. *The Politics of Reparations and Apologies*. New York, NY: Springer New York, 2013.

Periodicals and Internet Sources

Char Adams, "Evanston Is the First US City to Issue Slavery Reparations. Experts Say It's a Noble Start," NBC News, March 26, 2021. https://www.nbcnews.com/news/nbcblk/evanston-s-reparations-plan-noble-start-complicated-process-experts-say-n1262096

Julie Bosman, "Chicago Suburb Shapes Reparations for Black Residents: 'It Is the Start,'" *New York Times*, March 22, 2021. www.nytimes.com/2021/03/22/us/reparations-evanston-illinois-housing.html

Ta-Nehisi Coates, "The Case for Reparations," *The Atlantic*, June 15, 2014. www.theatlantic.com/magazine/archive/2014/06/the-case-for-reparations/361631

Jill Cowan, "Explaining the Reparations Effort," *New York Times*, June 3, 2021. www.nytimes.com/2021/06/03/us/explaining-the-reparations-effort.html

David Frum, "The Impossibility of Reparations," *The Atlantic*, June 3, 2014. https://www.theatlantic.com/business/archive/2014/06/the-impossibility-of-reparations/372041/

Nikole Hannah-Jones, "What Is Owed?" *New York Times*, June 30, 2020. www.nytimes.com/interactive/2020/06/24/magazine/reparations-slavery.html

Adeel Hassan and Jack Healy, "America Has Tried Reparations Before. Here Is How It Went," *New York Times*, June 19, 2019. https://www.nytimes.com/2019/06/19/us/reparations-slavery.html

Katanga Johnson, "US Public More Aware of Racial Inequality but Still Rejects Reparations: Reuters/Ipsos Polling," Reuters, June 25, 2020. https://www.reuters.com/article/us-usa-economy-reparations-poll/u-s-public-more-aware-of-racial-inequality-but-still-rejects-reparations-reuters-ipsos-polling-idUSKBN23W1NG

Thai Jones, "Slavery Reparations Seem Impossible. In Many Places, They're Already Happening," *Washington Post*, January 31, 2020. https://www.washingtonpost.com/outlook/2020/01/31/slavery-reparations-seem-impossible-many-places-theyre-already-happening/

Faith Karimi, "Their Ancestors Were Enslaved Workers. Now They're Getting $2,100 a Year in Reparations," CNN, June 27, 2021. www.cnn.com/2021/06/27/us/virginia-seminary-reparations-trnd/index.html

Kris Manjapra, "How the Long Fight for Slavery Reparations Is Slowly Being Won," *The Guardian*, October 6, 2020. www.theguardian.com/news/2020/oct/06/long-fight-for-slavery-reparations-evanston-chicago

Jameelah Nasheed, "What Are Reparations, How Could They Happen, and Why Do They Matter?" *Teen Vogue*, August 8, 2019. www.teenvogue.com/story/what-are-reparations-explainer

The New Yorker, "Ta-Nehisi Coates Revisits the Case for Reparations," June 10, 2019. www.newyorker.com/news

/the-new-yorker-interview/ta-nehisi-coates-revisits-the-case-for-reparations

Tina Nguyen, "The Awkward Truth About Democrats and Reparations," *Vanity Fair*, April 5, 2019. www.vanityfair.com/news/2019/04/2020-democratic-candidates-on-reparations

Akin Olla, "America Is Finally Acknowledging the Tulsa Race Massacre. The Next Step Is Reparations," *The Guardian*, June 3, 2021. www.theguardian.com/commentisfree/2021/jun/03/america-is-finally-acknowledging-the-tulsa-race-massacre-the-next-step-is-reparations

Andre M. Perry and Anthony Barr, "To Restore North Nashville's Black Middle Class, Local Policymakers Should Pursue Reparations," Brookings Institution, July 2, 2021. www.brookings.edu/research/to-restore-north-nashvilles-black-middle-class-local-policymakers-should-pursue-reparations/

Aaron White, "Reparations Would Shake Up American Capitalism—and That's a Good Thing," Open Democracy, May 25, 2021. https://www.opendemocracy.net/en/oureconomy/reparations-would-shake-up-american-capitalism-and-thats-a-good-thing/

Index

A

Adenauer, Konrad, 97, 98
affirmative action, 21, 48, 62, 65, 81, 132, 145, 146
American Descendants of Slavery, 57
apartheid, reparations for, 109–120

B

Bailey, Anne C., 34–37
Bayer, Patrick, 61, 62
Ben-Gurion, David, 98
Berry, Mary Frances, 134–135
Biden, Joe, 34, 74
Black Lives Matter, 16, 64, 65, 66, 136, 139
Bleakley, Hoyt, 75
Booker, Cory, 31, 32, 49, 54, 56, 129, 141
Bouie, Jamelle, 74
Bush, Cori, 65

C

Carter, Jimmy, 145–146
"Case for Reparations, The," 16, 36, 73, 95, 128
Castro, Julian, 47, 49
Charles, Kerwin Kofi, 61
Civil Liberties Act, 20, 37
Civil Rights Act, 36
Coates, Ta-Nehisi, 15, 16, 17, 22, 36, 48, 50, 52, 59, 73, 74, 95, 128, 129, 131
Collins, Chuck, 58
Commission to Study Reparation Proposals for African Americans Act, 22
Conyers, John, 16, 22, 51, 54, 73, 129, 139, 141
Craemer, Thomas, 57, 91–94

D

Darity, William "Sandy," 25, 32, 35, 56, 57
Dawes Plan, 105, 106, 107
Desai, Mihir, 149–156
Douglass, Frederick, 35, 130, 138
Du Bois, W. E. B., 20

E

Edsall, Thomas, 62
Eizenstat, Stuart E., 141–148

F

Fair Housing Act, 65
Feldman, Lily Gardner, 95–100
Ferrie, Joseph, 75

Field Order 15, 15, 16, 27, 35, 124
Floyd, George, 37, 64, 73, 122, 126, 139
Forman, James, 16, 21
"forty acres and a mule," 20, 27, 35, 55, 124, 148
Freeman-Woolpert, Sarah, 64–68

G

Garvey, Marcus, 36
Gary, Willie E., 58
Germany, 19, 20, 26, 43, 63, 95–100, 105–108, 132, 135, 141, 142, 143, 144, 153
G.I. Bill, 27–28, 51, 123
Great Depression, 27–28, 107
Gross, Terry, 122–127

H

Haiti, and reparation payments to France, 92
Hamilton, Alexander, 63
Hamilton, Darrick, 25
Hammond, Samuel, 59–63
Hannah-Jones, Nikole, 122–127
Harriet Tubman Community Investment Act, 28–29
Harris, Kamala, 31–32, 47, 49, 54, 59, 129, 161
Hickel, Jason, 57
Hillard, Graham, 46–48
Historian of the US Department of State, 105–108
Hollings, Ernest, 20
Holocaust, reparations for, 20, 26, 43, 95–100, 135, 141–142, 144, 153
Homestead Act, 15–16, 28
House, Callie, 35–36
Howard-Hassmann, Rhoda E., 101–104
H.R. 40, 34, 54, 69, 74, 129, 132, 139, 141
Hughes, Coleman, 154

I

International Covenant on Civil and Political Rights, 159

J

Jamaica, British reparations paid to, 40–41
Japanese Americans, reparations for, 20, 26, 37, 101–102, 135, 144, 146, 153
Jeffries, Hakeem, 32
Jim Crow era, 25, 35, 36, 46, 60, 69, 73, 95, 103, 104, 136, 138, 139, 149, 150
Johnson, Andrew, 16, 20, 27, 35, 124, 130, 148
Johnson, Lyndon, 21, 145

K

Kalambokidis, Theodore, 69–72
Kerner Commission, 21
King, Martin Luther, Jr., 21, 32–33, 67, 130, 137

L

Lee, Sheila Jackson, 34
Lincoln, Abraham, 15, 16, 27, 35, 93, 124, 147, 148
Luxembourg Agreement, 20

M

Marshall Plan, 26
McCloy, John, 97
McConnell, Mitch, 91
Moffett, Luke, 42–45
Moore, Audley/Queen Mother Moore, 16, 36
Morrison, Toni, 136–137

N

Native Americans, reparations for, 26
N'COBRA, 36, 139

O

Obama, Barack/Obama administration, 22, 32, 62, 143, 146
Obama, Michelle, 32, 103
O'Rourke, Beto, 47

P

Pelosi, Nancy, 49
Perry, Andre M., 24–33

R

Ragland, David, 64–68
Ray, Rashawn, 24–33
Reagan, Ronald, 37, 135, 144, 146
Rector, Robert, 85–89
Reparation Agreement, 95–100
Richburg, Keith, 82
Richmond, Cedric, 34
Ridge, Ashley, 109–120
Roosevelt, Franklin, 27, 28, 37, 107
Rosewood, Florida, reparations for, 104, 153, 155

S

Sanders, Bernie, 54, 59, 129
Scott, Joyce Hope, 136–140
Sharett, Moshe, 95–96
Sherman, William, 15, 20, 27, 55, 124, 147–148
Shinnar, Felix, 95
1619 Project, 122–127
slave owners, reparations for, 27, 35, 91, 93
Social Security, 27, 28, 51, 86
South Africa/apartheid, reparations for, 109–120

Sowell, Thomas, 78
Spath, Stefan, 77–84
Sunkara, Bhaskar, 128–132

T

Taifa, Nkechi, 57
Tanner, Michael, 46
Teixeira, Mimi, 85–89
Torpey, John, 19–23
Truth and Reconciliation Commission, 65, 109–120, 147, 153
Truth-Telling Project, 64–68
Tulsa Riot Race Massacre, 55, 149–156

U

universal basic income, 85–87
Universal Declaration of Human Rights, 159

V

Véliz, Carissa, 38–41
Versailles Treaty, 19
Voting Rights Act, 36, 145

W

Walker, Corey, 73–76
Warren, Elizabeth, 47, 48, 49, 54, 129
Washington, Booker T., 150
wealth gap, 22, 24, 25, 26, 28, 29, 31, 33, 54–56, 58, 60–61, 94, 122–127, 129
Wilkinson, Francis, 49–52
Wittmann, Nora, 138
World War I, 19
World War II, 19, 20, 26, 28, 37, 100, 101, 108, 135, 143, 144, 153

Y

Yanklowitz, Shmuly, 133–135
Young Plan, 105, 107–108

Z

Zhao, Raina, 54–58
Zook, Darren, 157–161

